The Adventures of Pixie Piper

A Fairy's Breath

Maricel Jiménez Peña

The characters and events portrayed in this book are fictitious. Any similarity to real persons, living or dead, is coincidental and not intended by the author.

Cover Illustration by Laura Diehl www.LDiehl.com
Illustration Copyright © 2014 by Laura Diehl
Author photo by Mariela Álvarez Xiloj

ISBN-13: 978-1497481497

DEDICATION

To my parents, because you never said no
to a notebook and a pen.

1

Cold Dreams

Pixie opened her eyes uneasily. Her head throbbed in pain. The walls around her were made of smooth polished ice. Her hair had gotten wet somehow and was now frozen solid, poking her in the back. She tried to move, but massive ice chains tied her arms and feet to the wall. The links burned her wrists and she could hardly feel her fingers. She looked up, but there was nothing but an icy, dense fog. She could hardly see anything at all. She squinted her eyes trying to see better, but a sudden gust of cold air shot at her in the darkness. She felt her lungs freeze shut. Nothing was getting through. She tried to force the air into her, but it was as if the air had somehow solidified. There was no hope. She was choking! Out of the blue, she felt someone nudge her gently.

"Pixie," said a familiar voice. She turned her head toward the sound, but there was nobody there. "Pixie," said the voice again. It sounded closer this time. "Pixie!" Someone was shaking her. "Wake up."

She opened her eyes and rubbed her face. Her mother's green eyes were staring back at her with a worried glint. "Are you feeling all right? You were shivering in your sleep," her mother said, feeling her forehead with the back of her hand.

"I'm ok mom. I guess the air conditioning was a little cold last night." She didn't want to whine to her mother about the dream. It wasn't the first time she had it. In fact, it was the third night in a row.

"Are you sure?" her mom insisted, checking her forehead one more time.

Pixie nodded.

"Well then, come get your breakfast. It's

waiting for you in the kitchen," said Mrs. Piper, and she hopped off Pixie's bed and left the room, closing the door behind her.

Pixie hugged her knees and rubbed her fingers. They were still numb from the dream. Better just get moving and shake the cold away, she thought.

The kitchen table was the exact same scene it had always been since Pixie had any memory. Her father sat at the corner where he had a complete overview of the kitchen. His face was mostly invisible behind the newspaper, except for his eyebrows and the top rim of his eyeglasses. On his plate, there was a half eaten serving of scrambled eggs heavily doused with ketchup, some bacon, and toast.

Her mother moved around the kitchen almost constantly, taking a cold mug of coffee from place to place. Pixie had never actually seen her eat breakfast, only make it.

"Hey Pixel," her father said winking. It was his pet name for her. "I heard you woke up shivering this morning. Are you feeling sick?"

"No daddy I'm fine," she flashed a look at

her mother. Why did she always make a big deal out of everything?

"Are you sure?" Mrs. Piper interjected. "Maybe you should stay in today, I don't want you to get an asthma attack."

"No!" Pixie almost fell off her chair. "It's the last day of school. There is going to be a party." She used her most humble face on her parents.

"Ok, ok," her father conceded.

"But she should at least wear a sweater," her mother pressed. "She could be catching a chill."

Pixie bit her tongue and ate her breakfast in three gulps in case her mother came up with a new excuse not to let her go. She had barely gotten up from the table when her mother spoke.

"Don't forget the sweater Pixie," she said.

Oh! Yes; the sweater. How could she ever forget to wear a sweater in eighty-degree weather? Sometimes her mother was just plain ridiculous. She ran to her room, grabbed the first long sleeved garment she could find and put it on over her shirt before going to the front door.

2

The Man In The Fuzzy Suit

Marissa Collins sat on the steps right below the big "G" of the Gardenville Elementary School sign. Her blonde hair was braided behind her back in one long plait. When she saw Mr. Piper's SUV she stood up and walked towards the curb.

"Hey Pixie," she said, her blue eyes scanning anxiously from side to side. "Do you need some help?"

"No, I'm fine Misa. What's wrong?" Pixie asked. There had to be something wrong. Misa was always worried about something.

"There is a strange old man watching the

school. He was here when my mother dropped me off and I saw him again about five minutes ago. He was wearing a weird fuzzy yellow suit and kept glancing through the windows."

"He's probably some student's grandfather," Pixie said casually. She wasn't going to let Misa go on a paranoid trip on the last day of school. "Let's just go inside." She took Misa's hand and pulled her up the steps.

A banner by the entrance said to go directly to the auditorium so the two girls turned left and walked down the long corridor. The party was decorated with a beach scene to remind the students the summer vacations were about to begin. Mrs. Vega, their homeroom teacher, was serving juice at the end of a long table full of party favors. She put two cups full of red liquid in front of them and went on to fill some more cups.

"What is it?" Pixie asked uneasily.

"Oh! Don't worry Pixie," Mrs. Vega replied. "It's one hundred percent juice, no artificial anything. I know your mom won't let you drink any other kind so I made sure there was some just for you. The rest of the table I'm not so sure about. Drinks were my department," she explained.

"It's ok Mrs. Vega," Pixie said. "I brought some snacks of my own." Pixie could never eat anything at a party. Her mother's list of forbidden foods was longer than Marissa's hair.

"Do you have any extra snacks?" Misa peaked into Pixie's bag.

"Sure. Do you want one?" Pixie knew how much Misa liked her mother's homemade granola bars. They were made from dry oats, sweetened with honey, and sprinkled with almonds.

"Thanks Pix," Misa said between bites. "These are the best! Your mother should sell them." She took the last bite and closed her eyes, savoring it. Then as she opened them, her eyes went dark.

"It's him!" she said, pulling Pixie close. "The man I told you; the one with the fuzzy suit." She was shaking.

"Calm down Misa! You're digging your nails into my arm," Pixie said. "I don't see any old man."

"There. Next to the exit door," she replied.

A short, stuffy man with white hair and a curly mustache leaned against the wall right below the exit sign. He wore a yellow fuzzy suit that made him look like a giant ball of pollen.

"Like I said, he's probably somebody's grandfather." Pixie said.

"Oh, really? Then how come I haven't seen him talk to anyone here?" she insisted.

"I don't know Misa; probably because you haven't been looking at him ALL the time." Pixie was starting to get annoyed. Sometimes Misa was worse than her mother. "Let's just have some fun. It's the last day of school!" She led Misa away from the exit, towards the rest of the party.

* * *

By the end of the school day everyone was heading back home. Pixie waved hello to Mrs. Collins.

"Do you want us to give you a ride, Pixie?" Misa asked worried. She knew how Mr. Piper was always late to pick her up.

"It's ok, Misa." Pixie said. "But, thanks anyway."

For some reason, her dad always forgot

where he put his keys, or his glasses, or whatever, just when he was about to leave. It made him late for everything. Pixie was used to it by now. She was always the last one to leave the school.

Right across the street from the school there was a small wooded park. On the edge, close to the sidewalk, a large tree with bright orange flowers spread its branches. Pixie sat on a bench beneath it. It was where she usually waited for her dad. The spot felt peaceful and whenever Pixie sat there, she felt relaxed, like nothing could happen to her. She closed her eyes and breathed the fresh aroma of the tree. It made her forget how late her father was. It was almost five o'clock. He was nearing his record.

She glanced around the empty school entrance. The gates were already closed. She was starting to regret refusing Misa's ride. By now, she could be home having a snack.

She looked at the park behind her, wondering what lay beyond the first line of trees. Maybe there was a whole world filled with adventure simply waiting for her to walk into it. But she would never know. Her mother had forbidden the park. Pixie didn't know why and her mother never explained. Not even her dad understood.

"It's a dangerous place," she would say.

But it wasn't. Many of the other kids in school had gone camping with their parents to that same park. Nothing had happened. They all said the place was safe. But Mrs. Piper didn't care. She simply did not want Pixie going there. Oh! Well! Pixie thought. There's probably nothing there but a couple of benches anyway.

A few minutes later, her father pulled up to the curb. "I'm sorry I'm so late," her dad began. "I couldn't find my glasses."

"It's ok, dad." She climbed into the car and took one last glance at the park and the tree. Even if it were simple benches, she thought, that would be enough adventure for her. Her father pulled away from the tree and eased the car onto the road. A ruffle of leaves from a nearby bush caught her eye. She wasn't sure, but she could've sworn something yellow stepped out of the bushes.

3

A Knock On The Door

The front yard of the Piper home was the envy of the entire neighborhood. Everything Mrs. Piper planted grew like Mother Nature had planted it herself. From chrysanthemums, to heliconias, to the tomatoes growing on the vine, she seemed to have a hand for growing things.

"Hello girls," Pixie said as she walked past the flowerbeds.

Mr. Piper smiled. "You're just like your mother," he told her.

Pixie shrugged her shoulders and headed for the door. Inside, the smell of fresh baked banana bread filled her nose. She dropped her bag right by the door and headed toward the kitchen. Her mother was sitting on a stool, cold coffee mug in her hand. She had flour in her fingers and some on her hair. When she saw Pixie, her face lit up.

"How was the party?" she asked.

"It was great," Pixie said. "Misa says 'thank you' for the extra granola bars."

Mrs. Piper smiled. "No problem. Maybe I'll bring her some banana bread tomorrow. I'm sure she'd like that."

Pixie agreed. Misa liked everything her mother baked or cooked. She was Mrs. Piper's #1 fan.

"Maybe I should take it to Mr. Collins right now," Mr. Piper said, walking into the kitchen with the phone in his hand. "He just called an emergency meeting at the office. I have to go."

"What happened?" Mrs. Piper asked worried.

"I don't know. It's strange, he just texted that we needed to meet in the office ASAP."

"But dad, we just got home!" Pixie protested.

"I know, sweetie, but I have to go," he said. "It must be big. This hardly ever happens." He grabbed his keys and began searching through the drawers. After looking in three different places, he found his wallet and walked out the door.

"I guess it's just you and me, Pix," her mother said comfortingly. "What do you want to do?"

"It's ok, mom. I think I'll just take a shower now," she said, walking to the bathroom.

After the shower, Pixie got dressed and went to the kitchen to get a snack. She was scrambling up the counter to get to the cookie jar when she heard a knock on the door. She ignored it. She wasn't allowed to answer the door anyway. She was halfway through a cookie, when there was a second knock. Apparently, Mrs. Piper still hadn't answered the door.

"Mom," Pixie yelled. "There's someone at the door."

For the longest moment, there was an eerie silence in the house. Then there was another knock. Pixie decided to go see who was at the door. She grabbed a step stool from the kitchen and used it to look through the peephole.

Whoever was at the door was fussing over the doorbell, and all that Pixie could see was the back of a yellowish suit. It looked like it was made of hay, or moss, or something. Suddenly the doorbell rang. Pixie almost fell off the stool. She caught her balance and looked again. The man had straightened up. Pixie could see him clearly now.

Her heart began to beat hard against her chest. She felt the palms of her hands start to sweat. It was him! She was sure of it. He had the same weird curly mustache, the big round stomach, and the fuzzy suit. It was the man from the school! The man Misa had been worried about.

Was Misa right all along? Who was he? Why was he at her house? She was sure she had never seen him before and she knew all of her parent's friends. Didn't she?

"Hello, Pixie," the man said smiling at the peephole. "May I come in?"

If her heart had been racing before, now it was about to explode right out of her chest. How did he know her name? Who was he? She searched her brain for pictures of old relatives and friends, but she was sure she had never seen him before that day at the school. Besides, she really didn't have that many relatives.

She jumped off the stool and started towards the hall to her parent's bedroom. Behind her, she heard the "click" of the bolt in the door. As she turned to look, the handle moved, the door jerked open, and the man in the fuzzy suit stepped inside the house.

4

What The Man Who Wasn't a Man Told Pixie Piper

Pixie screamed. Misa was right. The man in the fuzzy suit was about to kidnap her! And where was her mother? She must have heard Pixie scream. The woman had baby monitors all over the house, just to keep taps on Pixie. Where was she?

"Calm down, calm down," said the man. "I'm not going to hurt you. Geez! It's getting so hard lately. You kids are all getting too jumpy." He brushed some dust off of his suit and stretched out his hand with a bow. Pixie wasn't sure, but she could've sworn the dust had some sparkle in it. "Now, let's do introductions," he said casually. "My name is Daedalus Shortglow, but you may call me Dalu, if you like."

Pixie didn't know what to think. Could it all be some sort of joke? What sort of a name was Daeda… What was it again?

"I'm sorry sir," Pixie said, trying to be as polite as possible. "But who are you?"

"Why; I'm your fairy godfather, of course," he answered.

"My fairy god-FATHER?" Pixie said bursting into giggles. This had to be some sort of joke.

"Oh! I get the same thing from all of you!" he complained. "You can't just be happy you have a fairy god something, it has to be a MOTHER too?" He stomped his foot hard against the floor and made an ugly face, but it only made Pixie laugh louder.

"What do you mean all of you?" she asked forgetting she was supposed to be frightened.

"Yes, all of you," he repeated, a stern look about him. "I'm currently the godfather of 657 children and each and every one of you has laughed in my face the first time you see me. It really is getting quite humiliating. I have half a mind to apply for early retirement. And these days it's getting worse! Not even the little ones believe anymore. You're all too busy with your video games and DVD's. Ugh! It's enough to dull even the brightest fairy."

Fairy? She thought. That's when Pixie noticed there was a natural glow in him. It seemed to emanate from under his skin. And when he turned around, pretending to leave from offense, she saw he had two small, oval-shaped wings on his back. It wasn't surprising she hadn't seen them before. You see, fairy wings are usually so translucent you only see them when the light hits them at the right angle. And then all you see are tiny sparkles like dew drops in a spider web. It was these sparkles Pixie was seeing right now. They were suspended in the veins of Dalu's wings looking like floating diamond droplets.

Maybe she was asleep. She wasn't sure. But an old man fairy, wearing a yellow suit made of moss seemed unlikely. It had to be a dream… or a joke. And in both cases, it was best to play along.

"657 children you said; why so many?"

Pixie asked.

"We used to have a smaller workload. Back then, each child had at least one dream come true before adulthood, but there are ever so much more children now. It's crazy! I admit, some cases have 'fallen through the cracks' as you might say, but personally, I put my heart into every child I keep," Dalu said emphatically. "Now," he continued, "we must be off!"

"Off where, why?" she asked nervously. Maybe it wasn't a joke or a dream. Maybe it was worse. Maybe he was here to kidnap her after all. She could just picture Misa having a heart attack all the while saying: "I told you so."

"Why Pixie, I'm here to make your dreams come true, of course!" Dalu said. "It's what fairy god-parent's do, you know? And as my records state, you, young lady, have been dreaming of having an adventure for quite a long time now."

It was true. It's what she dreamed of most in her life. Difficult to do when your mother kept you indoors for less than two drops of rain.

"But, why me? Why now? I mean, if you have all those other godchildren…" she protested.

"Well, I'm actually on a special assignment and they've delegated my 656 other children amongst the rest of the god-fairies. I'm all yours 'till your adventure is over," Dalu said smiling.

"And why would they do that? I don't see why I'm more important than the rest of the kids," she said.

"Well that's obvious, isn't it?" he told her. But it wasn't obvious. Pixie looked at him with a puzzled face. "Oh! Dear!" he said realizing. "I forgot. You don't know, do you?" Dalu asked.

"Know what?" Pixie's voice was barely a quiver. Maybe she was sick and dying and that's why her mother never let her eat anything or leave her sight. Maybe that's why she was all of a sudden getting her dreams come true. It was a death sentence.

"Pixie," Dalu said brightly. "You are a Fairy!"

5

The Isle of Dahna

Now Pixie was certain this was all some masterfully elaborated joke. Her, a fairy, please! It was the most ridiculous thing she had ever heard. The old man had to be crazy.

"I can't be a fairy sir, I don't have wings," she said politely.

"Oh! Don't be silly. Sure you do! They haven't come out yet because you didn't know you had them. Anyway, not all fairies have wings," he explained, sprinkling her back with dust.

Suddenly, she felt an itch between her shoulder blades. Four wings erupted from under her skin, struggled with her t-shirt and finally tore the fabric in the back. They were huge! The top ones extended a couple of feet above her head, while the other two almost reached the floor, dripping a trail of golden purple dust all over the place. Like Dalu's, they were full of tiny veins that were covered by a thin, almost invisible film which sparkled in the light. She beat her wings a little. They shimmered, creating a dim light around her. Then, just like that, they began to wither until they were hanging limply down her back.

"What happened?" she frowned. "I can't move them at all!" What was the point of having wings if she couldn't use them?

"Don't worry. It's quite normal." Dalu assured her. "Wings are very strong, yet very delicate. Lack of use can be one of its worst enemies. You have never used yours and they have been cramped inside your back for all your life. But it's nothing a little exercise and stretching won't cure," he added. "Anyway, it doesn't matter. We won't be flying today. I've been issued a car!" His eyes grew big and his glow increased again. Golden fairy dust fell through his fingers as he rubbed his hands together in anticipating delight. "Shall we go?" he asked offering her his arm.

Pixie bit her lower lip. She was probably dreaming, but what if he was an evil fairy or something like that? She needed proof.

"How do I know you're not lying to me?" she demanded, pulling her hand away from his.

"Well I guess you have a right to ask, considering how things are these days," Dalu said fumbling through his coat pockets. Finally, he pulled out a thick green wallet made of the same material as his suit. As soon as he opened it the moss of the wallet began changing color, fading slowly into a yellower shade. "Here, these are my credentials." He handed her an id card from the Department of Faeries and Godchildren and a badge made of glistening white opal. It had the shape of a tree carved in the middle. Pixie had never seen anything like it. It had to be official.

"What about my mother? She'll worry about me," Pixie said.

"Oh! Don't worry about her. She will sleep until we come back from the Isle of Dahna," he said.

"The Isle of Dahna?" Pixie asked.

"Yes. It's where we're going," Dalu explained. Pixie bit her lip, not sure of what to do. "Let's go. You can see for yourself," he reassured her.

The street was completely deserted except for a bright red mustang convertible parked right in front of her house. It was clearly Dalu's car, which showed why he'd been so excited about it. Too bad the day was dreadfully rainy; otherwise they could've ridden with the top down. Pixie had always wanted to ride in a convertible, but having the top up somehow didn't count.

She clicked her seatbelt into place. The tires screeched as Dalu slammed down on the accelerator and headed towards the highway. Pixie watched the speedometer shoot past eighty. Her fingernails dug deep into the tan leather edges of the passenger seat. Dalu cut past several cars and made a sharp turn, almost hitting a brown van.

"Ouch!" Pixie rubbed her forehead. The force of the turn had been so strong it slammed

Pixie's head against the window. It didn't bleed, but a large pink patch atop an even bigger bump was on her brow by the next turn of the road. Daedalus slowed down after that, but five minutes later he was back over eighty and the ride became a nightmare from then on. Appropriately, Pixie closed her eyes, determined not to see the moments before doom.

When she finally opened them, they were parked near the school, right in front of her favorite tree. Dalu stepped out of the car and started walking towards the entrance to the park. The same park she was forbidden to go into.

"Where are we going?" she asked him.

"To the brook," Dalu answered, opening the rusty metal gate that led to the park. "If we catch the right current it will take us straight to the island."

"Dalu, what are you talking about?" Pixie said, wondering if Dalu was proving to be crazy after all.

"Fairies live in the Isle of Dahna, Pixie," he said, walking beside her. "There are many ways to get there, but my favorite is the brook. We ride the currents until we reach the island's shores."

"There is an island in the middle of a brook in the forest?" Pixie questioned, stopping to wipe some of the mud off of her tennis shoes.

"The Isle of Dahna is not in any particular place. It exists suspended between worlds. Any body of water can get you there as long as the conditions are right," Dalu explained.

Pixie was wondering what those right conditions were when they reached a small grove of mango trees. Dalu searched the floor and picked up a canoe shaped leaf. He inspected every side and vein and then laid it on a small trickle of water that flowed near the roots of the tree. With a wave of his hands, Pixie was splattered with fairy dust. Everything became a swirl of gold. She couldn't see anything. A heavy cloud of dust flew around Dalu and Pixie like a small tornado. Gradually, it began to grow bigger and stronger, until she was almost blown away by its force. When it finally dissipated, they were riding on the mango leaf, as small as ants, and the brook had become a wide flowing river. Each current, about eight to ten of them, flowed in a different color or shade.

"How do you know which is the right current?" Pixie asked.

"It's the green one, always the green one," he replied guiding their small boat with two long poles. He struggled for a moment and the boat took in a little water, but soon Dalu managed a strong push and they floated up to the green hue, latching onto the flow immediately.

It rode lazily, bumping off a rock here and there, but otherwise keeping a steady course. Ladybugs, caterpillars and all kinds of insects sailed on similar looking boats along the other currents. Pixie could see the others moved much faster than theirs, as if for some reason their green flow had no hurry to get to where it was going. Yet the real reason is that you never see the little things while you're in a hurry. They pass you by in a haze. You have to pace yourself in order to enjoy the details around you and only then can you get to Dahna. Cluttered, stressful minds can never make it. Either they miss the current or somehow they lose their way. That's why it's always easier for children; their minds have yet been preoccupied by the mundane.

With the rocking of the boat Pixie fell fast

asleep. The brook will often do that to you. There hasn't been one visitor who's been awake all the way through the boat ride. Some say if you don't sleep you don't make it, but that's just some silly folk tale.

When Pixie woke, the green flow had faded and they were drifting in circles. Three turns later, along the exact same path the boat had been floating before, she felt the leaf scrape the bottom of the river. As soon as the boat stopped, the fog disappeared and Pixie saw the sun shining brightly on the island.

They were standing on a white sandy beach with clear blue water. A trio of mermaids lay in the sunlight, casually combing their long locks of green and orange hair as they sang beautiful, yet unintelligible tunes.

Mermaids love to sing; especially around humans. For some reason, sailors just can't help steering their boats toward mermaid music, and seeing as they are usually laying around on rocks, that's where the boats end up crashing on.

Behind the beach was a tall snow-tipped mountain with a vast forest around it. Rainbows hopped from tree-top to tree-top forming a series of brightly colored highways.

"Welcome to the Isle of Dahna," Dalu said smiling.

6
The Royal Tree

As soon as they were off the boat they headed toward the forest. Dalu walked briskly, with a mix of flying and walking.

"Where exactly are we going?" Pixie asked, struggling to keep up with him.

"To The Royal Tree, of course. It is the home of The Queen and the most important fairy offices," Dalu explained.

"Is it far?" Pixie was beginning to get tired.

"No, no, no," he said. "It's just behind these ferns over here." And he pushed the ferns aside with his arm and stepped into the leafy shadows.

Dalu simply disappeared. Pixie looked around. The ferns were not big enough to hide an entire person, much less a whole tree. But then a hand with a yellow sleeve appeared from within the shrub and crooked its finger, signaling her to follow. Pixie hesitated, but then took hold of what she could only hope was Dalu's hand.

She took a step forward and felt the leaves brush against her arms and legs. The next thing she knew, the sky was ablaze with sunlight. They were in a circular clearing in the forest, and in the middle of the grassy field, there was an enormous tree. The trunk was as wide and thick as a building, with folds of roots that disappeared into the earth. In between those folds there was a set of doors embedded into the wood. Two rows of beautiful fairies (unless otherwise specified, all fairies are really beautiful) dressed in silver armor and helmets with green plumes guarded the entrance. The first one on the left saluted Dalu and gestured the others to let them through. They opened the path for them. As she walked, Pixie noticed the guards staring at her wings, which dragged across the floor leaving trails of dust everywhere. One of them didn't even bother to hide his laughter. Pixie was horrified! Dalu cleared his throat and they all straightened up in quiet formation.

"First to my office," he said turning to the left as they crossed the entrance. "I must get your file before we meet Ceres."

Inside, there was a grand atrium with stairs and tunnels carved into every bit of wall. Dalu grabbed Pixie's hand and took off into the air. He hovered in front of a tunnel and then flew into it at full speed. An air current pushed them even faster. In no time they had reached a small receiving area. There was a sign above two wide doors in the center of the back wall. It read: "Department of Fairies and Godchildren, making dreams come true, one child at a time". A young fairy was complaining to the attendant behind the counter, all the while glancing at two small children who sat on a love seat covered with red moss.

"What am I supposed to do with them? They're not in the system!" she kept saying nervously. The other just nodded and handed her forms to fill out.

Behind the door the office was teeming with life. Fairies kept popping up here and there with files and small hermetically sealed jars where wishes were collected in order to preserve their freshness. Long rows of desks filled the main room and the walls were covered in wish jars from top to bottom.

Dalu's office was through a door at the end of the room. The walls were adorned with hundreds of pictures of children, his favorites, for they didn't all fit in his tiny corner office. A slim area was left free for a bookcase carved right into the wood of the wall. His best tittles were all there: *How to build a dream, Into the Mind of a Child, Encyclopedia of Children's Worst Fears, (Vols. 1 & 2)* and *The Structural Design of a Wish and How to Make it a Reality.* All books Dalu felt should be in every god fairy's library.

He shuffled through the contents in a drawer of a file cabinet. After he checked in all the drawers he turned to the mess on his desk. It was a miracle if he found anything there. The piles were stacked so high you couldn't see him sitting behind it. "Here we are," he said. The brown folder was overflowing with parchments, pictures and orange post-it notes.

"What exactly do you do here?" Pixie asked.

"When babies are born, we assign a fairy to watch over them and make their wishes come true," he said looking up at her from behind the stacks of papers. "All wishes need to be approved by the Chief Executive Wish Officer. That's me."

"Do all children get their wishes?" she asked.

"Technically, yes," he replied.

"Even the bad ones?" she inquired.

"Yes. Sometimes, the bad kids need a wish come true more than anybody else," said Dalu, looking thoughtful.

"Why is that?" she asked, more intrigued than ever.

"Because bad kids aren't really bad, they just don't have anything good around them, so all they know is: bad. Besides," he added, "even the good kids behave badly sometimes."

Pixie felt him stare knowingly at her. She remembered the times she sneaked off from her napping mother and decided it was best to change the subject.

"So who is Ceres? You said we were meeting her," she said.

"Oh! Yes. Ceres is the Queen of the Fairies," he said. "She wants to meet you personally."

"Why?" Pixie asked a little worried.

Dalu frowned. It was only for a second, but Pixie saw it. "Let her explain to you herself," he finally said.

7

Pixie Meets The Queen

By the time they reached the Queen's private chambers Pixie was so nervous her wings were shaking. It was the most they had moved since they first came out and now she wished they would stop. Standing by the massive moss covered door, she searched her mind for what to say. It was empty. She felt her stomach churn and swallowed hard as Dalu pushed the living door.

Pixie stepped through the doorway into a soft bed of rich green grass with tiny blue flowers. The Queen's rooms were to the right beyond an archway covered with Morning Glory vines that hung from the ceiling. At the end of the garden there was a red toadstool table with white spots. Smaller golden mushrooms were used for seats. Fruit bearing vines hung from the walls filling the room with the fresh sweet smell of berries and brightly colored birds flew about eating to their hearts content. To the left was a pool of naturally warm water fed by a trickling waterfall that cascaded over the edge of the wall. A ray of light fell over the pool from a skylight above. It formed a tiny rainbow with the mist from the waterfall.

Pixie placed her open hand against her brow to shade the sun and take a better look. She was sure she had seen something standing at the edge of the waterfall. It was a fairy. The sun shone on her long white hair, revealing streaks of rainbow highlights that reflected off of her wings. The tall, slender figure held her hands together over her head like she was ready to jump. She flexed her knees a little, but stopped short when she saw Pixie. "Welcome home," she said glowing intensely. Then she flexed her knees again and took a splendid dive into the pool below. Her landing was flawless, and when she emerged from the pond, drops of water rolled down her figure and disappeared into the grass beneath her feet, until she was almost dry.

"Is that the Queen?" Pixie asked, feeling awkward with the word. She had been expecting an old, stern lady sitting on a throne with an oversized crown on her head.

"Yes," Dalu whispered, shushing her afterwards.

The Queen wrapped herself in a giant paper-like leaf and walked over to them. She eyed Pixie from top to bottom, pausing discretely at her dragging wings.

"Your Majesty," Dalu began after clearing his throat. "May I present…"

"Pixie," The Queen said. Her voice sounded like a chorus of bells. She ran over to Pixie and hugged her. "I have been waiting so long to meet you!" Then she turned around and spoke to Dalu like Pixie wasn't even there. "What's wrong with her wings?" she asked him. "They look much too frail to lift anything, much less fly."

She hasn't been able to move them since

they came out. I believe it may take months of training before she can fly confidently."

"She has exactly two weeks Daedalus. Then, she has to go back and she won't get a chance to practice."

"Wait a minute!" Pixie rudely, yet with reason, interrupted. "I can't be here for two whole weeks. What about my parents? They are going to worry about me. And my asthma; I didn't bring my asthma medicine."

"Mind your manners child!" Ceres said infuriated. "Your parents will be just fine. Time spins differently in Dahna. It will be no more than an afternoon nap. They won't even know you were gone. And what is this asthma you keep talking about?"

"It's a breathing problem," Pixie began.

"What breathing problem?" Ceres opened her eyes wide. "No fairy can have breathing problems! What is your mother doing to you? Keeping you locked indoors?" the Queen asked.

Pixie could only nod quietly.

"I see," Ceres said. "No matter, you'll have none of that asthma in the fresh Dahna air. I have no doubt about that. Now go learn to fly," she instructed, waving her and Dalu off with her hand.

Dalu looked at Pixie and padded her on the shoulder. She wondered if he knew how much she hated when adults spoke of her like she wasn't even there. As far as first impressions were concerned, this Queen had not made a good one on Pixie.

8
The Flying Lesson

Dalu took Pixie back to the beach for a flying lesson. A couple of mermaids sat near the shore, chatting away in mertalk and making jewelry out of seashells and pearls. Pixie waved at them, but neither finfolk took any notice of her; or perhaps they pretended not to, because they raised their voices so loud it did not seem like a coincidence.

"Don't mind them," Dalu told her, wrinkling his nose at the mermaids. "Most of them don't bother with the fairies. They think we are inferior because we cannot breathe under water. If you ask me, they are the inferior ones;

lying around all day doing nothing. With all their power, you would think they would do something more productive."

"What is their power?" Pixie asked. She had never believed in any of these mystical creatures, not really; much less expected them to possess any kind of real power.

"Mermaids are the rulers of the ocean and all that resides within it," Dalu explained. "And as you know, three quarters of the earth are covered by the sea. So the merpeople control three quarters of the earth."

"Well, they can't fly. Can they?" Pixie asked.

"No they can't. And neither can you. So enough with the chit chat and let us get started," Dalu ordered.

The flying lesson was rather boring. You see, fairies learn to fly the way babies learn to walk. They try and try gradually mastering each step and strengthening their wings. After the first year they begin to lift off the ground and stumbling from branch to branch they manage to get places, but it takes at least another year to finally free fly (that is: fly freely for long distances). Pixie wondered how she was going to do it all in so little time. Especially since her wings were too stiff to move. She had to be able to move her wings before she could try anything else.

Dalu tried tickling the spot between her wings. Pixie's wings shivered slightly, but nothing more. Then he tried moving them forcefully with his hands. It proved pointless.

"Is it possible your wings are handicapped forever?" Dalu said aloud. "I've never seen anything like this before. The stiffness should have gone away by now. Maybe your wings were born like this and no one ever knew. A genetic anomaly of some sort…"

"What?" Pixie asked. "You said it happened all the time. That it was normal." A surge of blood ran up into her face making her skin hot and her eyes itchy.

"It IS normal… when it gradually goes away," Dalu explained. But your wings just seem to be getting tighter by the minute. I can't do anything about it. Maybe if we wait until tomorrow…"

But Pixie had stopped listening. Her wings were crippled. She would never be able to fly. Somehow something always managed to land in the way of her happiness. She threw herself face down on the sand and began to cry.

"What's wrong?" said a boy's voice.

She looked up, and saw a fairy boy with dirty blonde hair and green eyes staring down at her. He was dressed in dark green banana leaf overalls and carried a bow and arrow on his back. His legs and feet were caked with clay and he looked at Pixie, quite surprised to see a young fairy crying.

"I can't move my wings," she told him between sobs.

"Oh! Can I see?" he asked, offering to help her up.

The boy stood behind her and examined her wings intently like he was some sort of wing doctor. After what seemed like a long time he delivered his diagnosis: "Your wings are dehydrated. Something's cutting off the circulation."

And indeed there was. Although the wings had torn Pixie's shirt, the holes were very small and they were too tight around the wing joints. With the blade of one of his arrows, the boy widened the holes in her shirt and immediately Pixie's wings began to expand.

"Thank you. Thank you. Thank you!" Pixie jumped up and down celebrating. She was about to hug him when she realized she didn't even know his name. "Who are you?" she asked suddenly.

"My name's Epime…Epim…Epimenides. But I can't even say it, so everybody calls me Meni," he said. "My dad is a wing doctor. That's how I knew how to fix your wings." A wide smile spread across his face.

"Thank you, young sprout," Dalu said to the boy. "Now Pixie, we can continue our flying lesson,"

"Flying lesson?" Meni asked surprised. "You mean you don't know how to fly?"

"Hey! I just found out I was a fairy today!" she snapped.

"Oh! I'm sorry," he said a little bashfully.

"There's really nothing to it. You use your top wings to lift yourself and the bottom ones to steer, like this," and he slowly lifted himself a couple of feet to show her.

She tried beating her wings, and to her surprise, they went so fast she even heard little bells ringing. There was a swirl of purple and gold around her and she began to glow. She felt her feet lighter and when she looked down, she saw they were just barely touching the ground. She got so excited she stopped beating her wings and dropped to the sand like a sack of potatoes. Meni laughed. One of her bottom wings was tangled with her foot and she was having trouble getting up. He bent over to help her, unraveling the strip of wing.

"Guess that's how you got that big lump on your head, huh?"

Pixie rubbed her forehead where she hit Dalu's window earlier. It was easily twice its normal size. "No," she said, flashing a nasty look at her fairy godfather. "That, we have Dalu to thank for."

"Come on, I'll have you flying like a fairy in

no time!" Meni said, stretching out his hand. She took it and they both began to beat their wings. Once again Pixie lost concentration, but Meni was holding her up this time.

"Don't worry, before you know it, you won't have to think about moving them at all," he said reassuringly. "Now hold on," and he shot up towards the sun, dragging Pixie with him.

She beat her wings as hard as she could, but she was too terrified to know who was doing the actual flying. Meni did several cartwheels in the air. Now she knew it wasn't her flying. After that he brought her back down near the edge of the forest and settled her on a branch. She was so dizzy she almost fell.

"Sorry about that," Meni said. "I just wanted to get us away from Daedalus. He'll never approve of what I'm about to show you. Besides, it's not safe to learn near the water. If you get flown off course or something you could land on the water. And when your wings get wet, they might get too heavy to fly. It's much better to learn here, in the forest where there is plenty to hold on to in case you fall."

He showed her his vine game. All she had to do was swing from vine to vine using her wings to carry her between the dangling plants. If she ever got tired or scared, there was a something to hold on to.

Pixie grabbed a vine and began beating her wings as hard as she could. She felt her body begin to rise and the weight lift off of her feet. Excited, she beat her wings faster until there was so much dust it was like trying to see through a thick fog. She couldn't even see the tips of her fingers; much less a far away vine that she could switch to. Terrified, she stopped beating her wings and let herself slide down the long vine back to the ground.

"Don't worry," Meni reassured her. "When you start going a little faster, the dust stays behind you and doesn't get in your eyes."

To ease her nerves, Meni tied a long vine around her waist. It did the trick. She beat her wings and felt her body being lifted again. Although the dust blinded her again, this time she didn't panic. With her arms above her head and her eyes firmly closed, she kept on going until she reached the branch above her. On and on she went until she was standing on the top branch of the highest redwood tree.

The view was magnificent. The tree was almost level with the tip of the mountain behind the forest. She wasn't sure, but it looked like the mountain was hollow inside; like a crater. Meni would surely know more. She turned around half expecting to find a ladder with which to climb back down. Suddenly she was paralyzed with fear. How on earth was she going to reach the floor? She didn't know how to fly downwards and she certainly couldn't just climb down. There were no footholds. She was so high up that she couldn't even see the bottom of the forest. The thin vine tied around her waist would probably break from the force of a fall.

"Meni, Meni!" she screamed. "I can't get down."

He was there in an instant. "You just beat your wings slower, so they'll slow your fall," he told her, helping her descend. "You can also spread out your wings like an umbrella, and if you're falling too fast, just beat until you're stabilized. It's not that hard; really."

But, Pixie was too scared to fly anymore. She held on to Meni like she had clung to her mother when monsters used to come to her room. The flight down seemed to take forever. When he finally settled her on the floor her body was shaking all over.

"Hey, don't worry about it. It happens to everybody," he said. "Come; let me show you something that might make you feel better."

He took her to the nursery. A small tree perched high on a rock with nests made of moss and hay safely nestled within its branches. Hundreds of little baby fairies laughed and gurgled inside them. Others were stumbling all over trying to master their flight. On a solitary nest, at the edge of one of the lower branches, was a small fairy a little older than the rest. She had golden hair down to her shoulders and light green eyes. Although she was bigger than the rest, it was clear that she was way behind on her flying. Every few minutes she would rise up in the air only to come crashing down on her padded nest; and every time, she picked herself up and tried again. Sometimes, she would beat her small fists against the hay of her bed or let out a low whimper, then her head would shake no and she would be up again beating her wings harder than the last time. Meni took Pixie closer and she noticed the little fairy had a broken wing.

"She was born like that," he told her. "Dad says she may never fly, but everyday she gets up and practices. She could hardly move an inch only a short time ago, and now look; she rises several feet in the air! Good job Minnie!" he told her as he flew down to greet her.

"When I reach the next branch, I'm going to try flying forward!" she said excitedly, glowing brighter than any other fairy in the nursery, sheer determination in her eyes.

Pixie felt a pang of guilt hit her squarely in the chest. Only minutes before she had been feeling hopeless and crippled and had almost given up on herself. Now as she faced Minnie she realized the only disability had been in her mind. If you think you can't do something you won't be able to. She had given up too quickly. And only on her first try. You can never succeed if you just give up. So she asked Meni to take her back to the vines. She flew up to the top of the tree (without the vine tied to her waist) and then jumped!

It wasn't as hard as she thought. Once she had conquered her fear she learned how to fan out her wings and use them like a parachute; the way Meni had explained. She was descending quite smoothly with this technique when there was a sudden gust of wind. It blew her sideways, sending her spinning out of control.

"Aaaah!" she screamed, desperately flinging her arms in hopes of catching something. But her hands missed the vines around her and she was falling, helpless!

9
Fly

Pixie spun around in the air as she plummeted down at an uncontrollable speed. The wind blew against her face so fast it was hard to keep her eyes open. Squinting, she looked from side to side hoping to find something she could grab hold of, but all she could see were leaves and golden dust. Her arms flung about blindly, brushing past nothing but fresh cool air. "Meni!" she screamed. She had flown up the tree and forgotten all about him. But why didn't he follow her? He should have been up there with her.

Suddenly, she felt the sharp sting of a thin branch slapping against her face. Her hands reached out for it. A mess of fern-like leaves broke in her grasp. Then another branch scraped her thigh. She was probably getting closer to the ground. She had to do something fast. Pixie began beating her wings as hard as possible, taking long deep breaths. Maybe that way she could stabilize herself.

Her body dove relentlessly. The wings didn't seem to do anything at all. She beat them harder and harder until the little bells were all she could hear. She hovered in the same spot as if suspended from an invisible string. Then she shot upwards, leaving a long trail of gold and purple dust behind her. The wind blew hard against her face, washing away all her doubts and fears. She looked down at the floor as it got further and further away. She was flying! She was really flying!

"Bravo!" Meni clapped slowly and loudly from a tree close to her landing spot.

"Where were you?" she demanded, remembering how afraid she had been only moments before. "I could've died!"

"But you didn't," Meni said, a mischievous

little grin on his face. "Besides, I was right here to catch you if you didn't help yourself."

"Help myself?" Pixie cried. "What if you missed? You're crazy. I am never taking another lesson with you, Meni," she declared waving him off as she walked in the opposite direction. It wasn't long before she realized she had no idea how to get back to the beach. When she turned around, Meni was right behind her.

"Are you ready to start flying forward now?" He asked, still grinning at her in an arrogant way.

"It seems I don't have much of a choice. Do I?" Pixie said. "After all, you have me trapped in your own little section of the forest. Don't you? Are you going to let me fly into a tree next time?"

"Oh, come on; stop being angry at me and start feeling proud of yourself. You flew all the way to the top of the highest tree in only one flying lesson. I believe that's a record," he added with a wink.

All of a sudden, Pixie felt triumphant. She flew! How many kids in her school could say that? It began to dawn on her that she was actually very lucky. She was having her very own adventure. The kind you only find in books or movies. It would be a waste of time to be angry during any of it. Not when she could be flying around. She smiled. A warm sensation filled her whole body, especially her hands. They were glowing, bright and yellow, and as she smiled wider, the light spread up her arms reaching almost to her face.

"Let's fly!" she said, rising up to the nearest branch. Meni followed. He showed her how to use her bottom wings to stir her direction. Before long, she was flying forward across several feet. By the end of the day her wings were burning. She was sure they would quit on her any second. That's when Meni decided it was time to call it a day and they flew back to the beach.

"Where have you been?" Dalu yelled at them. "I have been worried sick! Are you all right Pixie?" He spun her over making sure there weren't any extra scratches on her. "I was beginning to think the boy was a spy. And as for you, young Epimenides, you are never to see Pixie ever again!" he said glowing scarlet.

"But Dalu," Pixie protested. "Look." She

beat her wings, elevating herself a couple of feet off the floor and flew about fifteen feet across the sand. Dalu's jaw dropped open. "Please let Meni keep teaching me," she pleaded.

Dalu never actually replied. He only nodded quietly staring at Pixie in disbelief.

10

The Rainbow Ring

Dinner will be served on the mushroom table in the garden at eight O'clock sharp. (There is a Timekeeper on the wall next to the door). You will find proper attire in the wardrobe beside the bed.

Ceres

The wardrobe was embedded into the wood like Dalu's bookcase. The doors were carved with the image of the Royal Tree in the middle so that each door contained half of the picture. Inside there were a series of dresses all made from flower petals or delicate leaves. Hanging on a hook on the inside of the door was a fancier dress with a note attached.

Wear this.

The skirt of the dress was made entirely of rose petals. Several layers of petals overlapped fading from a deep rose to a light pink on the top. The bodice consisted of two large white rose petals that were held in place by a series of pins. How am I supposed to put this on? Pixie wondered. She had managed to put the skirt on right, but for all she tried the pieces of the top kept falling off.

"Darn it," Pixie cursed, struggling with the pins in the dress. "I'm really going to be late."

"Do you require some assistance," said a soft almost inaudible voice from a doorway that led to the rest of the chambers.

Pixie froze in her tracks. The doorway was cast in shadow and all she could see were a pair of feet dressed in white socks and wooden Japanese sandals.

"Who's there?" she asked, trying not to shake. Whoever it was, they hadn't made a sound. For all Pixie knew, the person could have been standing there all along.

"I am Tilly," said the girl, stepping into the room and out of the shadows. Her small feet inched along the floor, barely showing beneath the mustard colored kimono that covered her from head to toe. As she walked, she never raised her eyes from the floor. "I will help you with the dress if you like," she said without looking at Pixie. Her head hung so low Pixie could hardly see Tilly's face; only the dark, ebony shine of her hair.

"Yes, I really need your help," Pixie told her, grateful that help had suddenly appeared even if it had been a little spooky.

Slowly and quietly Tilly removed all the pins and spun the white petals around, pinning them together on the sides. "There," she said when she had finished. "You must go now. The Queen doesn't like to be kept waiting." With that she turned about and left the room as silently as she had entered.

Pixie took one last look at the timekeeper by the door. Eight twelve. The Queen was probably going to yell at her. The least she could do was make a grand entrance. She walked into the garden tall and straight like she had learned in ballet class.

The Queen sat by the table, sipping from a long-stemmed flower. "Good evening Pixie. You look absolutely beautiful," she said. "Come. Sit right here beside me and tell me all about your flying lesson."

Pixie sat on the mushroom next to Ceres, but before she could get comfortable, servants appeared from all directions bearing several large trays of food. A fairy with a bit of a blue hue to his glow began lifting the covers of the plates one by one; releasing the most incredible aromas Pixie had ever smelled. Fresh baked tulip bread with butter, spring salad with rainbow dressing, fall roots with orange leaf sauce, and dew drop ice cream with tree bark cookies for dessert. And the best part; everything was completely natural!

"How did you know?" Pixie asked.

"Know what child?" The Queen asked back.

"How did you know I couldn't eat anything artificial?"

"Fairies can't eat anything that isn't 100% natural. Doesn't your mother explain things to you? It can be fatal! Our systems can't tolerate anything artificial. It can kill us!"

"Oh! I see…"

"Oh! Don't worry darling. Eat up without worries. Everything here is Fairy proof," Ceres said, digging her fork in her plate.

When the meal was over and the servants had taken all the trays away, Ceres reached into a fold in her dress and retrieved a small wooden box.

"This is for you Pixie," she said, handing the box to her.

There was a silver ring inside, with an oval shaped stone in the middle that shimmered with all the colors of a spectrum. When she took it out of the box Pixie felt a peculiar warm-cold sensation.

"It is a Rainbow Ring," said Ceres. "We use them to cast rainbows."

"Wow! Thank you!" Pixie replied staring wide-eyed at the ring.

"I was supposed to give it to your mother when she got married, but …" The Queen paused for a moment, doing a bad job of hiding her sadness; then she choked back the lump in her throat and smiled. "I think it's time to break the tradition. I will give it to a blossoming granddaughter instead."

11

Family Secrets

Pixie wasn't sure if she had heard right. Did The Queen say something about her mother? "I'm sorry," Pixie began, "whose granddaughter?"

"Pixie," the Queen said, taking her hands into hers. "You are my granddaughter."

"No," she protested. "'Abue' is my grandmother."

"I am your other grandmother," the Queen explained; "your mother's mother. I have wanted to meet you since you were born."

"But my mother said you died," Pixie insisted. "It can't be."

"Yes," Ceres said casting her eyes down. "I'm afraid your mother and I had a... disagreement, and she left the Isla of Dahna to live as a human in the outside world."

"A human?" Pixie asked. "What do you mean live as a human?"

"Because she's a fairy too, of course," the Queen said emphatically.

"What?" Pixie started going back to her dream theory. There was absolutely no way that her mother was a fairy. It was impossible. Not someone who was always so scared and worried.

"Why else would you be a fairy, Pixie?" she asked. But Pixie could only stare in silence trying to see if she believed it all. "Come," said the Queen. "Let me show you something," and she gestured Pixie to follow.

They walked through a flower curtain and into a small corridor carved into the wood of the tree. On the left wall there was a picture of a little girl. It looked almost exactly like Pixie, except her hair was lighter and there were small dots of sparkle circling her face.

"That is your mother when she was about

your age," Ceres told Pixie. "Her name is Delmes."

It was amazing. They looked so much alike, Pixie could hardly believe her eyes. She had never seen a picture of her mother when she was a child. She realized there was a lot she didn't know about her mother. She seemed to have a whole life Pixie was unaware of.

"But she doesn't have wings, she never speaks of it. How could she just leave her whole world behind?" Pixie finally asked.

"She has forgotten. It is what usually happens in such cases. When fairies forget who they are, their wings retreat back into their bodies and slowly wither until they are crippled. With each passing day the memories of fairy life drift away," Ceres explained. "Eventually they stop producing dust all together and the transformation to human is almost complete. All that is left at that point are a pair of vertical scars between the shoulder blades."

The scars, Pixie thought. She had asked her mother about them once when they were at the beach. Mrs. Piper told her she had fallen off a tree when she was a young child.

"That's just something that happened when she was a kid," Pixie told Ceres still disbelieving. "She's not a fairy. Besides, why would she want to forget any of this anyway?"

"Are you sure?" Ceres asked, tilting her head slightly to the side and sprinkling a tiny bit of dust over Pixie's hand.

Pixie stared at the shiny golden dust in her hand. It glimmered in the light almost electrically, reminding her of something from long before, but she wasn't sure what. Then suddenly she remembered. When she was very little, the ceiling of their house began to shed a strange sort of powder. Mr. Piper had complained about it over and over again. It had been especially problematic in her parent's bedroom. Three different repairmen came to the house to try and fix it, but none of them could keep the strange golden dust from coming back. In the end, the problem went away on its own. Now, as Pixie stared at her shiny hands she realized what had been the dust all over the house. It had been fairy dust. Her mother was a fairy after all.

"Will she be able to be a fairy again?" Pixie asked.

"She's never really stopped being one," she replied. "She just chose to live a human life. She could look like a fairy again, have wings and all, but first she would have to remember and I don't think she's ready to do that."

"Why not?" Pixie asked.

Ceres rested her hand on Pixie's shoulder and let out a deep sigh. "Your mother was unhappy with my choice of husband for her, so she ran away. When she left, she met your father and never came back."

"Who was she supposed to marry?" Pixie asked nervously.

"Whom," Ceres corrected her. "She was supposed to marry a fairy named Garm," Ceres replied. There was a look of worry in her face. "But come, let's go back to the garden so I can teach you how to use your new rainbow ring."

Pixie didn't want to change the subject, but it was obvious the Queen did, so she decided to drop it. She could always ask Dalu about it later.

"How does the Rainbow Ring work?" she

asked, when they were back at the garden.

"Well, first you have to put it on," her grandmother said smiling, sad thoughts all gone from her face.

Pixie placed the ring on her right hand. It spun and danced around her finger with enough space for two.

"It doesn't fit," she mumbled, trying to avoid her grandmother's gaze.

"I think it fits just right," Ceres said. She took Pixie's hand and spun the ring around so that the stone was facing upwards. Instantly the ring shrunk until it fit snugly against Pixie's skin. "Now, whenever you want to cast a rainbow, you make a fist and aim with your arm straightened, like this," Ceres instructed, showing her the motion with her arms.

Pixie clenched her fist and pointed at the water. A bright rainbow shot out from the stone and arched its way to the pool. It was magnificent, each color sharply defined and forming a perfect semicircle! Now, no one can help trying to catch a rainbow. Once it's close, you can't fight the hand that yearns to touch it.

Automatically the arm reaches out, but you can never hold on to it. It slips like wet soap from your hands. Yet, that is exactly what Pixie did next. She tried, and the rainbow slithered away from her hand and settled close to the waterfall.

"Darn!" Pixie exclaimed.

"Oh! Pixie, sweetheart! You can't catch a rainbow," Ceres said laughing. "You ride it!"

She flew over to it; landing on tiptoes at the top, then threw herself down the side like a slide, splashing onto the sparkling pool. Once again the water seemed to have no effect on her and her head emerged from the pool almost entirely dry. Only a few drops like morning dew clung to the strands of her hair.

"It was one of my favorite games when I was a young fairy," she said, splashing water at her. "Sometimes my sister and I would ride rainbows from cloud to cloud, even all the way to the ground. The secret is not to touch it with your hands."

Pixie shot out another rainbow and flew towards it, landing on tiptoes as her grandmother had done.

"Pixie, you're flying wonderfully, and in just one day!" Ceres said, clasping her hands together and beaming at her.

Pixie smiled wide, showing all her teeth. She had been hoping the Queen would notice her flying skills.

They rode rainbows and splashed for several hours until both Pixie and Ceres were so tired they could hardly move. Pixie lay in her mother's old bed enjoying the soft steady crackling of the fire. The whole room was infused with the aroma of cedar and there was a hint of cinnamon from some stick Tilly had thrown into the fireplace. The scene suggested deep profound sleep, but Pixie could hardly blink. She had flown! She had a ring that could make rainbows and she was living in this amazing tree house. It was all starting to feel too good to be true. Why would anyone want to leave? She pictured her mother with fairy wings flying carefree through the garden. Somehow it didn't seem possible. How could someone who never let her daughter play in the rain come from a place like this? Maybe Dalu had made a mistake. Perhaps her mother wasn't Delmes after all and

Pixie had been adopted. But she couldn't get the shiny glimmering dust out of her mind. She had seen it. She had played with it. It had been her mother's. But how could her mother just forget? The thought crawled into her dreams that night. She dreamt she had forgotten who she was as a human and was wandering through the Isle of Dahna as an orphan fairy who couldn't remember her own name.

12.

A Fairy's Breath

The next day, Dalu gave Pixie a tour of Dahna. There was a large lake and a series of caverns to the South, the spring gardens in the East, where the beach and forest lay, a small desert in the West, and the mountain to the North. The mountain was really an old volcano that had cooled and filled with water over time. The effect was an enormous lake hidden inside the crater, so deep it couldn't be seen except from above. Long ago, back when the lake was still fluid, Hela Winters, the fairy Queen of winter, had acquired the property and turned it into a glacier where she carved a huge castle inside. It was heavily guarded by abominable snowmen and fierce ice snakes that slithered almost invisible through the snow and froze you with their bite. Hela was the mother of Garm, the fairy Pixie's mother was supposed to marry.

"I don't understand why the Queen was forcing mother to marry that fairy. If he was so bad, why did grandmother pick him in the first place?" Pixie was determined to get as much information out of Dalu as possible.

Dalu sighed deeply. "The fairy world is steeped in old traditions. It is customary that a fairy princess marries a fairy prince. In the case of your mother, the arrangement had been made long before Hela and Garm's evil became apparent." He sat down on a rock and gestured Pixie to sit. "I'm afraid it's a bit complicated," he continued. "You see, once a fairy is promised to another fairy, the contract is binding. That means it cannot be broken. Your grandmother couldn't break the betrothal even though she wanted to. Your mother's only choice was to run away and forget."

"But Dalu," Pixie asked. "Why was it so bad if Garm became king?"

Dalu looked at her tenderly and stroked the top of her head. "Hela Winters is the Queen of Winter. She controls that season. But your grandmother is the Queen of the Seelie Court, she is the Queen of all fairies. If Garm married your mother, he would've eventually shared the throne of the Court with her. And with all that power, he would've probably let his mother leave the winter on forever. The whole thing would've upset the balance of nature.

"If mom were Queen I'm sure she'd never allow that," Pixie insisted.

"My dear Pixie," Dalu warned. "If Garm should ever find your mother and become King, he would kill both of you. Lucky for everyone he shall never find her. Only a fairy's breath could find her."

"What's a fairy's breath?" Pixie asked curious.

"When a fairy breathes out air," Dalu explained, "it may be collected in a glass jar. If that jar should ever be opened, and the breath left to fly free, it would find its way back to the fairy that breathed it. No matter how far away that fairy was. All you would have to do is follow it."

"So how did you find me?" Pixie asked.

"I'm your fairy godfather. God fairies always know where their godchildren are. But I don't know where your mother is. Just you," he said.

"Oh," Pixie exclaimed. "But what if he has one of her breaths? I mean, they were betrothed and all."

"Unlikely. He would've used it by now. Besides, catching fairy breaths is no easy task. The only time we catch breaths is at the moment of a fairy's birth. It's easy then. A fairy's first breath is golden, like light, so we collect them and keep them in the Fairy Breath Registry. Like a birth certificate."

"So my mother is safe then?" Pixie asked. It seemed that her presence in Dahna could put her mother in danger. What if someone found out who she was? "Maybe I shouldn't have come here," she said worried.

"Nonsense. You just turned ten. Soon, you will be a teen. If kids don't get at least one dream come true before the teen years they become sullen and depressed. There was a chance your wings would never come out if we let that happen. Have you any idea what a depressed teen fairy looks like? They wilt like flowers my dear."

"I see," Pixie said, not really understanding.

Suddenly a guard fairy came rushing through the bush. He landed in front of Dalu and handed him a rolled up parchment sealed with a tree symbol like the one on Dalu's badge. Dalu took it and read it quietly. "Come Pixie. We must go," he said somberly, grabbing Pixie's hand and dragging her behind him as he flew in the direction of the Royal Tree.

They landed in one of the top terraces. Meni and the Queen were waiting for them. There was an empty jar in the Queen's hand and a very worried look on her face. The jar was marked *Delmes Brightwing*. Ceres handed Dalu the jar. He inspected it, trying to determine if the seal had been broken. It had. He looked at the Queen, and then, both of them together looked at Pixie in a way that sent shivers up her spine.

"Pixie," Dalu said in a shaky voice. "I'm afraid we have serious problems." He paused, breathing deeply and looking at Ceres. "Your mother's breath has been stolen."

13

What A Mother's Breath Can Do

Ceres and Dalu spoke amongst themselves all the way towards the Queen's chambers. Meni and Pixie remained behind trying to overhear their conversation, but Pixie could not understand a single word they were speaking.

"It's old *Faery* Dialect," Meni explained. "Only the elder fairies speak it. I'm afraid I don't really know that much, but my dad speaks it," he added. "Pixie, did I read right? Did it say 'Delmes Brightwing' on your mother's Breath Jar?"

"Yes. I think so. Why?"

"Because Delmes Brightwing isn't just any

fairy. She's the princess that was promised to Garm!" Meni began.

"Yes, Dalu was telling me about that. I still don't get why she left this place, even if that fairy was horrid."

Meni stopped walking and stood in front of her. "Your mother did one of the bravest things any fairy has ever done," he said. "Garm and his mother are horrible fairies! They are evil. Everyone says so. Your mother did the right thing leaving here." His eyes looked almost scared.

They reached the Queen's chambers and sat at the mushroom table near the pool.

"Pixie," Ceres began, "Dalu and I are extremely concerned about the safety of your mother. We are almost certain it was Garm who stole her breath and if he releases it, he will have a means of finding her. There is only one solution. You must be there when the breath is released and stop it!"

Pixie wasn't sure if she had heard right. It almost seemed like they were laying the entire plan on her shoulders. "Why me?" she boldly asked.

"I get it," Meni interrupted. "It's because it's her mother, isn't it? Because it is a Mother's Breath first and foremost?"

"Exactly!" the Queen replied. "Are you the young sprout teaching Pixie to fly?" she asked him.

"Yes, mam."

"Then you will help her with her quest," she declared.

"Will someone please explain to me what you are talking about?" Pixie demanded.

"You see Pixie," Dalu began, "a mother's breath will always go to her child before her own in any occasion. It is the way of nature and mothers. It is even more powerful than fairy magic. So if you were to be close to your mother's breath when it was released, the breath would go to you instead of your mother and Garm would never know where to find her."

"Great! So how exactly am I going to be close to it when they release the breath?" she asked sarcastically.

"We will sneak you into Hela's castle and hide you there until they release the breath," Ceres announced. "Now, for the moment I need you two to keep on practicing your flying while Dalu and I figure out the details of this mission. Remember not to tell anyone who you are Pixie. In case Hela has any spies around."

Pixie left the room feeling disoriented. Was she dreaming again, or did she actually sign up for some death defying fairy mission? The look on Meni's face was enough answer.

14

An Alternate Route

By the end of the week Pixie was flying like she'd been doing it from the day she was born. Their mission would take place on the New Moon. According to the Queen's intelligence crew, it was the most likely date of release, since the darkness provided by the New Moon guaranteed that Garm could see the breath and follow it. Pixie and Meni had explored the entire forest by then, and needing no more flying lessons, had decided to start exploring the mountain. It was another way of preparing for their quest.

They reached the edge of the forest where

the terrain began to slope upwards. The trees were sparser in this area, but there was still plenty of vegetation for them to move about well hidden from view. They went on foot until their path was cut short by a wall that shot straight up for hundreds of feet.

"This must be the edge of the mountain," Meni said. "We should walk parallel to it; make sure there are no guards. Who knows? Maybe we will be able to fly up this side unnoticed."

The gigantic mass of rock and dirt was icy cold and covered in black slippery moss. There were no plants growing on it. Not even a fern or ivy. The closest trees were easily ten to fifteen feet away from the wall. It was as if the forest knew it should keep its distance. Pixie didn't see any guard posts. Somehow they did not seem necessary. No living thing would willingly venture into such an uninviting place; no one except them. A deep chill began to creep up her neck. She couldn't wait to get out of there.

"Let's go back, Meni," Pixie told him, her voice barely audible.

"Yes. It's getting late anyway," he replied

quickly.

Pixie turned to take the forest path when something caught the corner of her eye. There was a dark slash, like a rift in the wall, a few paces ahead of them. "Do you see that?" she asked Meni pointing in the direction of the wall. "What is that?"

Meni squeezed his eyes. "It might be a cave. We should go take a look." And with that, he darted off towards it.

There was an opening in the wall! A small trickle of water flowed between the rocks on the floor and the most horrible stench emanated from within. "It must be some sort of sewer," Meni said.

"It certainly smells like one," Pixie noted.

"Do you think it might lead up to the castle?" Meni asked, a big grin spreading across his face.

"It has to," Pixie nodded. "We have to tell Dalu about this."

The two fairy kids went back to the Royal Tree. They ran into Dalu's office practically out of breath and making plenty of noise. Dalu was at his desk, hidden behind the mounds of files stacked on top of it.

"Excuse us Dalu," Meni mumbled. But Dalu took no notice of them and continued scribbling something into one of the folders.

Finally, Pixie walked up to the desk and pushed aside the pile that covered Dalu's face. "We have wonderful news!" she said.

Dalu jumped in his seat and almost fell backwards. "You scared me half to death Pixie!" he said frowning. "Fairies have been known to die of fright, you know?"

"But Dalu, we found a cave that leads into the crater!" she said excitedly.

"You did what?" Dalu asked sounding quite upset. "You were exploring the crater by yourselves?"

They both nodded quietly, looking down at the floor.

"You could have been seen! What if something happened to you?" As Dalu yelled, his glow became bright red and his breathing heavy. Then, just as quickly, he turned golden again. "Now, tell me about this cave," he said. "We must not let the mischief go to waste."

"Sir," Meni said, "I think it's some sort of drain or sewer from the castle."

"And why is that, Epimenides?" Dalu asked; an obvious tone of disbelief.

The sound of his full name made Meni shudder. His parents only used it when they were really upset. "Because it smelled like a sewer," he finally said, "and the walls were round like a giant tube."

"Really?" Dalu seemed interested now. "We will have to check the archives, then. Follow me," he said, walking out of the office.

He led them down a long dark shaft that descended below ground level. At the bottom, the air was musty and cold, and the walls were covered by dark wet moss. They walked down a narrow corridor that led to a vast cavern. The word "archives" was carved into the wood above the archway. Beyond the threshold, a small platform held a desk at the edge of a huge abyss that ended in darkness. The walls along the deep ravine were lined with books and scrolls. A short plump fairy with whitish purple hair held up in a bun greeted them from behind the smallest spectacles Pixie had ever seen.

"Hello Mrs. Root," Dalu said bowing a little with one hand behind his back.

"Why, hello Daedalus," Mrs. Root said cheerily leaning over the desk. She glanced at both Meni and Pixie and fixed her eyes back on Dalu. "It's been a long time since I've seen you down here," she continued. "What are you looking for?"

"Blueprints," Dalu replied without hesitation, "the ones for the castle in the crater."

"Why would you want those?" Mrs. Root inquired. "I hear that old Winters doesn't like having visitors. Besides, the prints on file are probably from the original design. I'm sure she's changed some things since then." Mrs. Root's eyes batted fiercely at Dalu.

"If you don't mind, Mrs. Root," Dalu said between gritted teeth. "I would like to see those blueprints."

Mrs. Root took a step back from the desk. The smile was gone form her face. "Well! Old age has certainly turned you sour, Daedalus" she snapped. "Let me see if I can find that for you. It might be quite difficult. There is a mess in the architectural section. I'm afraid some of the records have been misplaced."

Pixie didn't know Mrs. Root, but it seemed to her there was no mess in the archives. The old fairy was just being difficult to pay Dalu back for his rudeness. Fairies seemed to take everything quite personal.

Whether it was true or not, Pixie would never know, but Mrs. Root took more than an hour to find the blueprints. Pixie was surprised the lady brought them at all. By the time she gave them to Dalu his glow was crimson red. Pixie was sure he would yell at her or something, but instead he snatched the scrolls from her hand and left without saying thank you. A look of satisfaction was on Mrs. Root's face.

Back in his office Dalu spread open the prints. From the look of it, dozens of pipes ran beneath the castle. Small tubes led to bigger drains that collected the water from different parts of the castle. The big drains all emptied into a large collecting pool, which in turn flowed out of the crater through a single main tunnel. Judging from the position of the tunnel in the mountain, it appeared to be the cave Pixie and Meni had found. If the blue prints were correct, the second tunnel to the left of the collecting pool would lead them to a storage room where the breath was likely kept. After they infiltrated the castle they were to hide out near the breath until Garm released it. Then all Pixie had to do was breathe. Once that was done they had to fly out of there as quick as lightning, hopefully before anyone noticed their presence. It was an unlikely event, but one they would have to hope for.

13

The Treebarks

The day before the New Moon, Meni invited Pixie to dinner. The Treebarks lived in an old squirrel hole in one of the grand oak trees of the forest. Dr. Treebark, Meni's father, had built his practice on one of the branches, where he tended to dozens of fairies a day. He was well known in Dahna and everybody liked him. It was probable he had mended wings from all the families throughout his career and fairies never forget a helpful hand. In that sense, they can be quite loyal.

Mrs. Treebark was a plump, jolly-looking lady with bright red hair and green eyes. She was famous for her cooking. When she wasn't busy taking care of her nine children, she catered fancy fairy parties. In fact, she had cooked for the Queen on more than one occasion and received praise from Ceres herself.

"You must be Pixie!" Mrs. Treebark said excitedly as Pixie and Meni flew through the moss curtain that served as the door. "Meni has told us all about you. I finally get to put a face on the name. Come sit. Dinner will be served in a jiffy."

They sat at a round table that grew right out of the floor of the tree hole. It was so big, it easily accommodated twelve people, but Pixie was sure more could be squeezed in. The kitchen was in the right hand side of the room. Smooth, wave shaped counters grew out of the walls all with drawers and cabinets. There was no refrigerator, but Pixie noticed a strange plant that hung from a vine on the ceiling. It had a blue fruit shaped like a pear, but bigger than Mrs. Treebark. Meni's mother stood in front of it and pulled on a small leaf at the top. A slit appeared in the center and cool air began rushing out. She slid her hand through the gash and retrieved a large jug of freezing cold flower juice.

"It's an ice plant," she said, seeing the look

of surprise in Pixie's face. "Everything inside it is kept nice and cold."

Suddenly, there was a loud rumble coming from high inside one of the walls. Pixie looked up to see a collection of kid fairies, each smaller than the next, fly out of a hole, close to the ceiling. They spiraled down in single file like a perfectly orchestrated choreography and sat at the table next to Meni. The smallest one, Daffodil was barely bigger than Minnie from the nursery.

"So, Pixie is it?" asked the fairy sitting beside Meni. Her hair was a light shade of blue and her eyes sparkled with golden light. "Is it true you are a half breed?"

"Periwinkle!" Mrs. Treebark snapped. "That is not polite at all. Whatever happened to your manners, young fairy?"

"I was just curious," Periwinkle said in her defense. "Until a week ago nobody had heard of one for over a hundred years, now we have one sitting at our table." She sized Pixie up and down and then turned to her brother. "Not bad," she said winking at him. "She's cute."

"Shut up Perry," Meni said with a tight jaw.

Pixie noticed he was jamming his elbow on her side underneath the table.

"Hey! You don't have to hit me," Periwinkle yelled. "I was just trying to be nice."

"Well you're not doing a very good job," said Daffodil winking at Pixie from the other side of the table.

"Mind your own business Daff," snapped Periwinkle.

"Don't talk to her like that," said a boy's voice somewhere from the middle of the table. Before Pixie could put a face to it, the whole room erupted with loud yells. Wings began to beat and the table was covered in multicolored dust. It was impossible to see anything, much less understand what was being said. Suddenly, a strong wind began to blow and all the dust cleared up.

"That is enough!" yelled Mrs. Treebark. "Your father will be home any minute now and you will all be in your best behavior. Is that understood?"

Everyone went dead quiet and all nine fairies nodded silently in response. Pixie wondered if this was the way big family's behaved all the time. Her dinner table was usually very quiet. Even with all the fighting, it seemed better than the boring conversations her parents had during a meal.

Dr. Treebark arrived shortly after covered from head to toe in fairy dust; a consequence of mending wings all day. He kissed his wife tenderly on the lips and then sprinkled some dust on each of his children (a traditional fairy custom to ensure health and fortune). When he came upon Pixie he stopped short.

"Dear missus, do we have nine or ten children?" he asked eyeing Pixie suspiciously.

"Dad, this is Pixie," Meni said.

"Oh! Yes! Pixie, the friend you keep talking about. Delightful to meet you!" he said. "Meni told me how he fixed your wing. Wasn't that ingenious of him? He'll make a fine wing doctor some day!" He patted his son on the back, and then sprinkled Pixie with fairy dust as well.

Meni smiled automatically, but rolled his eyes and averted his father's gleam. Apparently he wasn't happy with Dr. Treebark's gloating.

Just then, Mrs. Treebark came over with a tray in each hand and one on her head. There was stardust seasoned roast turkey basted in summer juice and apricots, Dahnish muffins with pollen chunks, wild mushroom rice with garlic-rose nectar and daisy cheesecake for dessert. It was even more delicious than the meal with her grandmother. In the end she felt so stuffed she wondered how she would fly back to the Royal tree.

14
Stuffy Dreams

After dinner Pixie stood on the ledge of the Treebark home, staring at the dark forest that lay before her. Meni had promised to fly her back, but she could hardly keep her eyes open. She heard the sound of colliding beads and Meni appeared.

"I know what you're thinking. Too stuffed to fly, huh?" he said.

She nodded, but her thoughts were also on something else. "Meni," she began, "how come you forced a smile when your dad was praising you back there?"

"When?" he asked, pretending not to know

what she was talking about.

"Oh! Come on! Don't play dumb with me. You know, when your dad said you'd be a great doctor. You totally FORCED a big bright smile."

"He's always saying what great doctor I'll make someday. It drives me a little crazy," he said.

"What's so bad about that?" Pixie asked.

"I don't know. I like helping him out and learning all about wings, but I don't know if I want to do what he does all the time."

"Then, what would you like to do?" she asked.

"My friends and I always talk about competing in the F. E. X. Games," Meni whispered.

"The F. E. X. Games? What's that?"

"Shhhh. Not so loud. They're the most important fairy extreme sport event of the year. There's leaf surfing, vine flying, rainbow sliding, even dragon riding. It's awesome! My friends say I have a shot at the vine flying competition. It's like what I showed you on that first flying lesson except we do acrobatics and spins in between vine jumps. The winner gets 10,000 gold nuggets! But my dad will never let me compete. He says it's a waste of time and I could hurt myself."

Pixie nodded. She knew what it was like to have overprotective parents, although she doubted the Treebarks would qualify as such. "Have you talked to your mom? Maybe she can convince him to let you go," she suggested. "After all, this mission will be more dangerous than those games and they let you go, right?"

"They don't know about the mission, Pixie," he confessed. "They think I'm going to give you more flying lessons."

She was horrified. How would she ever explain it to the Treebarks if something should happen to Meni? For a moment, she regretted getting him involved in her mess. He should have told his parents where they were going. They had a right to know their son was about to risk his life for the sake of Dahna.

Meni gave her a knowing look and stopped her before she could utter a protest. He calmly reminded her how her parents knew nothing of her mission either and that she was about to risk her life herself. Pixie couldn't argue with him. Truth is she wanted him there. He made her feel much safer than Dalu (no offense to him) and without a friend to share her adventure it seemed rather pointless. So they said no more about it.

Grrrr, Pixie's stomach churned trying to digest all the food she'd consumed.

Meni laughed. "You can spend the night if you're too full to fly, Pixie. I'll send a bee message to Dalu," he told her.

She agreed. There was no way she would fly in the dark half asleep. She wasn't such an expert flyer yet.

Meni walked up the branch to a small beehive snuggled between the leaves. Moments later, Pixie saw a bee fly out of the hive and disappear into the forest. "There," Meni said. "Now we can go get some sleep."

Meni and the rest of the children slept in the room through the hole near the ceiling. It was cylindrical in shape with a high ceiling. About five feet above the floor there were three rows of rectangular holes carved into the wood of the wall, each with feather mattresses, pillows and small firefly lamps. Pixie would be sharing the lowest bunk with Daffodil.

That night she dreamt of her mother. She lay sleeping in the couch just as she had left her, when suddenly a wisp of air slipped through the window and dove into Mrs. Piper's mouth. Pixie yelled for her to wake up, but it only caused her mother to take a deep breath and swallow the air. At that moment Garm burst through the door, the crown on his head and a long wooden staff in his hand. He grabbed her mother and flew off into the cloudy night sky laughing maniacally.

Pixie woke in a sweat and almost fell off the bed she was sleeping in. She was shaking all over. Even though it was a dream, she knew it would come true if she failed. A sudden homesickness took over her. She missed her mother's blueberry muffins and the smell of her father in the mornings. She missed being tucked in and kissed good night. She even missed the sound of the *coquíes* back home; those little frogs that sang their names perched up on trees at night. A cold breeze blew in from the doorway below. It made Pixie shudder. She wrapped herself tighter with the blanket, but it would never replace her mother's embrace. She began to cry softly, afraid that she would never have those things again; that she would never go back home, or worse, that she would return to an empty house and find herself all alone. The possibility of failure was suddenly very imminent. What if they couldn't get to the breath on time? What if they were spotted? What if they were caught and forced to tell all about her mother?

She was frantic! "I'm just a little girl!" she thought. "They can't just lay it all on me!" Tears began to stream down her face again. The feeling of hopelessness was becoming overwhelming. She begged for sleep to come, something, anything to stop the sudden fear that had gripped her, but it didn't and with every passing moment she felt herself wondering if she should go back home and run away with her parents, abort the mission and leave the Isle of Dahna forever just as her mother had done years before.

15

Unexpected Complications

Pixie sat at the table puffy eyed and looking like a truck had run her over.

"What happened to you?" Meni asked making an ugly face.

"Nothing!" she snapped. "Let's just have breakfast so we can get this done and over with."

"Sorry," Meni said exaggerating his tone. "I didn't know you weren't a morning person."

Pixie flashed such an angry look at him that he sat down and didn't say another word until after breakfast. She ate hers just as quietly, spreading the mood throughout the whole table until everyone was chugging down their food in dead silence. By the time they had finished she felt slightly better, but by then the marigold waffles and flower juice were mixing with her lack of sleep and she felt worse than she had the night before. But she had resolved to go. The idea of running away had been stupid. She'd gotten enough sleep to see that, but the fear was still there. And the more she waited, the worse it became. The knot in her stomach tightened with every second that passed so she had resigned to getting through it as quickly as possible. Perhaps that way there would be no time to screw up.

They moved quickly and were at the Royal Tree before the sun was up, making their way to Dalu's office where they had agreed to meet. Dalu wasn't there, but he had left the leaf packs ready from the night before. They were filled with cloud bread sandwiches, a water pouch and cloaks prepped with holes for their wings. The blueprint to the sewer system was lying on his desk, notes scribbled on the margins. They put their cloaks on and waited for Dalu.

An hour went by and there was still no sign of him. Not even a bee message. According to the schedule they should have left by now. Pixie began to pace the room.

"Maybe he overslept," Meni suggested. "Perhaps we should go try and find him. Where does he live?"

"I don't know. He always comes to the garden," Pixie said, suddenly realizing how little she knew of Dalu. She thought it over for a while and came to only one solution. "We'll ask Ceres. She's the one who planned all this. She'll be furious when she finds out Dalu's late. Everything was carefully scheduled."

Ceres was still in her quarters having breakfast when Pixie and Meni burst through the mossy door of the garden. As predicted, she was outraged at Dalu's disappearance and sent out several servants to search for him. She admitted it was unusual of him to be late considering he was a perfectionist when it came to his job and Pixie thought she heard worry in her grandmother's tone. A fact, that didn't help calm her already anxious state.

About an hour later, the guards found Dalu in the Underwater Creature section of the library.

He lay unconscious on the floor, still in his robe and wearing his slippers. A gnome with a red hat and thick glasses that kept slipping off his nose was inspecting Dalu's arm.

"What happened?" Pixie asked terrified. Although she could see Dalu was still breathing, his face was strangely pale, with a bit of a green hue.

"I'm afraid Daedalus has been bit by a sleeping jellyfish," the gnome announced, tucking his long white beard under his green coat.

"A sleeping jellyfish, doctor how is that possible?" the Queen asked with a deep frown.

"You see that shelf with the sample specimens?" Dr. Oakstead said, pointing to the bookcase next to where Dalu lay. "And the jar with the sleeping jellyfish, right next to the one-eyed decapus? We found it, halfway open. The jelly was on the floor, next to Dalu. It's not strange for these creatures to keep their sting long after they are dead. See? There's the spot, right under his left arm." He held up Dalu's arm and lifted the sleeve of his robe. There were three red lashes near his elbow that were already beginning to bubble.

"Is there an antidote, doctor?" Meni asked, studying the lashes intently.

"I'm afraid not," the gnome replied, squinting his eyes up at them. "Once infected, a victim will sleep for the next fifteen to twenty-four hours. Nothing will wake him, not even fire or ice. But when it passes, he will be just fine, so there's really nothing to worry about."

"Nothing to worry about?" Pixie shouted, her arms slamming hard against the side of her thighs. "What are we going to do? We can't go without Dalu."

Ceres dismissed Dr. Oakstead before turning to Pixie and Meni. "Now children," she said looking at each of them squarely in the eye. Her deep blue eyes showed the same sadness Pixie had seen when the Queen spoke of her mother Delmes. "I know this is a very unfortunate incident, but this is the only chance we have. If Garm releases your mother's breath tonight, all is lost. You must go get the breath without him."

"But…" Pixie began. Meni placed his

hands on her shoulders and turned her to face him.

"We have to go, Pixie," he said, his tone deeper than she had ever heard it before. "We can't let Garm get your mother. She's your family."

"But what about Dalu?" Pixie protested, staring at the spot where he had lain.

"Pixie," the Queen said, kneeling down and looking into her eyes, "I don't think what happened to Dalu was an accident."

"What do you mean?" Pixie asked, staring at the floor like a zombie.

"Dead jellyfish don't just go crawling out of jars and stinging people," she said. "And if Dalu had stuck his hand inside the jar, he would have been stung in his hand, not his arm. Do you follow?"

"Yes!" Meni said excitedly. "And wouldn't the jar be on the floor as well?"

"Very likely," the Queen replied nodding her head at Meni.

"So someone must have set the sleeping jelly on Dalu," Meni continued.

"Exactly," said the Queen.

"But who?" Pixie asked, not sure she could take all this in at the moment. Why would anyone want to hurt Dalu?

"I don't know. One of Hela's spies I suppose," Ceres said. "I had my suspicions from the moment you said Dalu was missing. But don't you worry, when I sent the guards to search for him I also told them to seal off all the exits. The spy won't get far. Soon we'll catch who ever did this and pupate them for a hundred years," Ceres reassured her.

"What do you mean pupate?" Pixie asked, struggling with the word.

"It's the fairy jail," Ceres replied. "Bad fairies are locked up in a pupa for the duration of their punishment. A pupa is a cocoon like the butterflies make before growing their wings. While someone is pupated, they cannot move much and they can't receive any visitors. All they can do is ponder their crime."

"Are they good fairies when they get out?" Pixie further implored.

"Some of them Pixie," Ceres sighed.

"Others, I'm afraid, never turn good. I will tell you more about it when you return. For now, you must make haste. The new moon is only a few hours away.

16

More Unexpected Complications

The Queen double checked all their provisions and escorted them to the top of the Royal Tree where the main rainbow station was located.

"Now Meni," Ceres said when they reached the terminal. "You must take the mountain express. It will lead you straight to the skirt of the volcano. From there you follow the valley path, keeping the wall to your left until you find the tunnel. Do you have any questions?"

"No, your Majesty. I know what we have to do," Meni replied, bowing his head slightly. He looked so confident, Pixie wondered if she was the only one who was actually afraid.

"Good. Here are two gold coins for the rainbow." The Queen gave Meni a pair of golden coins. On one side, there was a shield with a cross in the middle. At each end of the cross was a letter corresponding to the four points of the compass. Within every section of the shield there were depictions of the four elements: earth, air, fire and water. It was the seal of the Seelie Court. On the other side of the coins, there was a picture of the Royal Tree.

"It costs a gold coin to ride a rainbow?" Pixie said astonished.

"You'll see," Meni said smiling mischievously.

The Queen looked at him rather sternly and then turned her eyes to Pixie. "You two take care of each other and stay together," she said.

Pixie wasn't sure, but she could've sworn her grandmother's voice was trembling. It's a strange thing to hear a Queen's voice quiver. It makes you realize they are just people like everyone else. On the other hand, Ceres' sudden vulnerability made Pixie very nervous. She clutched Meni's hand. It was cold and sweaty and he held hers tighter than she did his. Maybe he really was just as scared as she. But it didn't matter; they would have to rely on each other now; swallow their fears and trust their instincts.

Without a glance back, Pixie pulled Meni towards the information counter. A skinny fairy with orange hair sat chatting away into a conical shaped leaf. She paid no attention to either Pixie or Meni and continued her one sided conversation filing her nails meticulously as she spoke.

"Excuse me," Meni said. "Which gate for the Mountain Express?"

The orange haired fairy froze her hands and raised her eyes up to look at Meni. Then with a roll of her eyes she pointed towards a large sign about two feet away from them. All the gates were properly enumerated with their final destinations. The Mountain Express was at gate number five, at the end of the North Wing.

They passed several wooden carts filled with fresh fruits, flowers, seashell jewelry and all kinds of things fairies like to buy before travel. Next to the gate, there was a small fountain of fresh water that sprung right out of the floor. They stopped to take a drink and splash their faces. Pixie had never tasted water like that. It was delicious; cold and crisp with a hint of sweetness to it; certainly more refreshing than any thirst-quenching drink back home.

The gate was divided into twelve posts with rotating bars and slots for the coins. Pixie dropped her coin and pushed the wooden bar forward until it gave way, letting her through. A small elf-like man with a red beard and a green top hat greeted them and pointed to a pair of seats aligned to the yellow row of the rainbow.

"Fasten your seatbelts," said the man showing a golden tooth behind his friendly grin. "It's the blue button on the arm rest."

Pixie pressed the button and a silver sash stretched from one side to the other hugging her tightly by the waist.

"Ready?" asked the attendant.

Meni nodded at him and without any warning the seats shot forward gliding along the yellow path. They were going rather fast, but occasionally, they caught glimpses of the beach or the nursery tree in the distance. Then, the rainbow began to spiral downwards, gathering momentum. The colors began to spread out. Their road veered left around the trunk of a large tree and then gradually leveled out until they landed on soft green grass. The other colored roads exited to each side of them forming a semicircle around a large black cauldron where gold coins jingled as they landed from a hollow branch overhead. A little man, wearing buckled shoes and a green coat, stood on a platform at the edge of the pot counting the coins as they fell. They walked past him and out onto a clearing.

"So there is a pot of gold at the end of the rainbow," Pixie said glancing back at the leprechaun.

"Yes," Meni smiled, taking Pixie's hand and pulling her away from the exit.

The clearing was round and small. Only a few rays pierced the canopy overhead infusing the area with a warm golden green aura. On the root of a tree, right in front of them there was a small sign that read: "Lizard Taxi". Several lizards fitted with saddles were lined up one behind the other waiting to take customers to their destinations. A small wingless fairy with a purple orchid hat, mounted on the first lizard and it quickly scurried towards a tunnel nearby. Right across from the Lizard Taxi was a giant snail slowly pulling a cart full of children fairies. Meni walked past them and took a small path hidden behind a bush to the right.

The path led them straight to the edge of the mountain. In five minutes they had reached the sewer. The ground was wet and soft. Their feet sank into the mud making it difficult to walk and the stench was almost unbearable. They had gone only a few yards when they came to a large gate closed with several kinds of padlocks. Meni pushed and kicked, but it wouldn't budge. It was a dead end.

17
The Decapus

"What are we going to do now?" Pixie asked frustrated.

"I don't know. Check the map, maybe there's another way around," Meni said.

But the map was clear. Only the main pipe led outside and they were on it. This was the only way through. He sat down on a rock next to Pixie, staring at the goo beneath their feet. The whole floor was covered in it, even under the gate.

"Maybe we can dig underneath it," he proposed, bending down to feel the ground.

"Dig through this disgusting stuff?" Pixie said making an ugly face.

"Yeah! Unless you'd rather wait around for that gate to magically open," he snapped, feeling the ground for a place to start digging.

They began to paw at the mud near the bottom of the gate, but it was too watery and all the goo flowed right back into the hole.

"It's not working," Pixie whined, making one last attempt to dig. She felt her hand scrape the bottom of the metal bars. There was a wide space between the gate and the bottom of the swampy tunnel. They might be able to crawl through, but they would have to dive underneath the mud to do it. There was no point in thinking twice. She took a deep breath, closed her eyes, and plunged into the stinky substance, feeling her way around for the gate. There it was, right above her. She pushed with her feet, slithering through the gap. It was small, but with a little effort she was on the other side. Meni followed her, and moments later, muddy and wet they were on their way to the ice castle.

The drainpipe led them into a wide chamber with a lake. The water was pitch black and very still, almost like it was frozen. They veered to the right, following a rocky path along the edge. Pixie could see a circular opening where the pipe continued at the opposite end of the cavern. They walked towards it being careful not to slip on the mold covered rocks of the path. Meni reached the opening first. It was very dark inside so he shook his wings to create a bit of glow. Nothing happened. His wings were now caked with dry mud from going underneath the gate and no amount of beating produced any dust. Pixie tried with hers, but it was no use. The mud was making her wings so heavy she could hardly move them. In a stroke of genius she walked over to the water and dipped her wings inside for a rinse. Every muscle in her body stiffened. The water wasn't frozen, but it was freezing! She shook her wings hard, letting the water gurgle as it passed through the thin skin of her wings. Soon the liquid around her became infused with golden-purple light. Her wings were clean. She was half way out of the water when she felt something rub her leg.

"Ugh! I think a fish just swam by me," she said.

"Don't be such a girl Pixie, two minutes ago you were covered in sewer slime," Meni said annoyed.

"It's still disgusting!" she said, taking the last steps out of the lake.

Suddenly, something griped her ankle. It pulled with such force that Pixie fell forward. The grip around her leg tightened and she felt herself being dragged forcefully into the water. She screamed. An octopus-like beast with a single giant eye, eight tentacles, and two clawed arms held Pixie firmly while it lashed at Meni with its claws. It flung her to the side and she almost hit the wall of the cave. Meni managed to avoid getting caught, but now the one-eyed decapus was retrieving into the dark liquid of the underground lake with fresh lunch. She saw the water bubble as the giant beast began submerging beneath the cold liquid of the cave still waving her about. She struggled, but the decapus had a firm grip and with every move she made it seemed to only tighten its hold. It tossed her around as the rocky wall kept getting dangerously close to her. At any moment, one of those swings would send her crashing onto the jagged surface, if not, she would be taken under the icy water and drown. She had to find a way to get loose.

Pixie saw Meni grab his bow and arrow. She closed her eyes, hoping he could hurt the monster with it, but instead, the decapus smashed her down into the icy water and the angle of the fall burned her face almost raw. Excruciating pain ran from her face, along her spinal cord all the way to her feet as the beast pulled her out of the water. Pixie gasped for air just in time to be flung into the water once more. This time she landed sideways. The whole of her left side stung like a terrible sunburn. She caught another glance at Meni stretching the string in his bow to the maximum as he aimed the arrow at the decapus' gigantic red eye. The weapon shot out of Meni's bow and caught the monster right on target. She breathed a sigh of relief. The decapus would let go of her. Soon it would begin to loosen its grip. But as she felt herself slowly descending to the water, the animal's tentacle only held her tighter. The dying beast simply refused to let go of its prey.

Pixie took one last deep breath before she felt her body pierce the surface of the water. Her arms and legs pushed hard against the monster's tentacle, but to no avail. The decapus was cutting off her circulation. Before long, her limbs became so cold and numb she could hardly move them. Her vision blurred. There were flashes of dark water and suction cups as she slipped in and out of consciousness. She no longer felt the burning cold of the freezing lake or the strength of the decapus' grip. She caught one last glimpse of Meni's face distorted by the ripples in the water before her face sank. "I've failed. I've failed," she thought. And then everything went black.

18

Ice Cold Beauty

Pixie woke with the sharp warm sting of a good slap in the face. She was lying by the edge of the water, a chunk of tentacle still attached to her leg. Meni was hovering over her, dripping wet. He held a small dagger stained with yellow blood in his right hand. She coughed, spitting out a bit of freezing water. It numbed her throat and her entire chest in the process. There was a moment of panic when she thought her lungs had been paralyzed, but soon she was able to breathe again.

"Are you all right?" Meni said looking her over like a doctor again.

"I think so. Did you cut that monster's

arm off?" she asked.

"Ah ha," he nodded.

"Thanks."

"Anytime Pixie, that's what friends are for," Meni told her. "Now let's get going. It shouldn't be too far."

The tunnel continued in a straight somber line deep into the crater. It widened as they walked along. The small trickle of water that leaked from the lake had become a shallow river of dark, murky liquid. It was thick and sticky like syrup and the greenish brown color was no different to Pixie than the slippery goo of the sewers back home. The tube ended in a rectangular pool with several smaller pipes emptying into it from left and right. At the opposite end there was a brick wall covered in black mildew.

According to Dalu's notes on the map, they were supposed to take the second passageway on the left. It would lead them to a small storage where that breath was kept. They could hide out there until Mrs. Piper's breath was released. Pixie flew across the pool and reached the second opening. There were metal bars running from floor to ceiling. There was no way to get through. She checked the next pipe and it was heavily barred as well. In fact, all the pipelines were gated!

"Don't panic," Meni said coolly. "There has to be a way to get up there."

They checked the wall. Meni mentioned there could be a doorway or some stairs leading out of the chamber, but they found nothing. The wall was solid brick. Pixie lay against it. The cold damp moss that covered it was so slippery she almost fell sideways. Everything was going wrong. First Dalu suffers a freak sleeping jellyfish attack, then the decapus, and now this. Even if they found another way through, how would they ever find the breath room? She leaned her head back, ran her hands over her hair and let out a deep breath. Then her eye caught something round protruding from the center of the arched ceiling. She shot upwards. Her glow illuminated the whole room and she could see it was a wheel for an airtight door. It had to lead somewhere.

"Come give me a hand Meni. I think this is a way through," she called.

It took some effort, but finally they heard the loud creaks of rusty metal giving way as the wheel began turning. Meni inched the door open and peaked through the slit. There was absolutely no one in sight. All that could be seen were dark blue velvet curtains. Meni pulled himself up and then helped Pixie. They were in a small space enclosed entirely by the curtains. The floor was made of ice and there seemed to be no doors of any kind except the hole they had just come through.

"Where are we?" Pixie asked, her voice echoing slightly off the floor.

"I have no idea. But there has to be a door or something behind these curtains," Meni said. He walked over to them, feeling for an opening in the fabric. "We're inside the castle all right," he exclaimed.

The curtains hung over a wide rock in the center of a large pool full of penguins and white crocodiles. A low bridge made of light blue ice connected the rock to the rest of the room. It was vast, with gigantic ice columns carved with all sorts of winter animals rising up until they disappeared in a thick fog that lingered about twenty feet above the floor. A huge stalactite on the far left had been illuminated from underneath shooting out hundreds of tiny rainbows that reflected off the icy walls so the room was submerged in color.

Pixie pulled the curtain open a little further to get a better view. There was a throne adorned with diamonds and sapphires. Like everything else, it was made of light blue ice, but Pixie thought it was quite beautiful. There was no one sitting on it. The room was empty. Carelessly, she stepped out of their hiding place, pulling Meni with her.

"Wait Pixie," Meni whispered. "There might still be someone we haven't seen."

"There's no one here," she insisted. He was starting to remind her of her mother with all the worries. "Come on. You have to see this. It's beautiful!"

"Thank you. I'm glad you like it," said an icy voice from close behind her.

19

Hela Winters

The cold voice made Pixie cringe. Every pore in her skin had reacted to this awful voice like somehow it could remember it. She turned around to find Hela Winters smiling viciously at her, a pair of blue lips savoring its fresh caught prey. Pixie was paralyzed. She looked into the glacial eyes and found she could not pull her gaze away. Hela was beautiful and horrible all at the same time. She was long and slender, like most of the fairies Pixie had seen so far, except her skin was completely white, yet somehow faded, like it had been erased, and she had no wings. In her hand she held a staff made out of a long icicle with a rounded tip. She had long blue hair with silvery streaks. It fell loose against her bare shoulders. At the tip of each strand was a tiny icicle extension. When she moved, the tiny icicles collided together making light chiming sounds that reverberated off the glacier walls. The only jewelry she wore was a delicate crown made from giant snowflakes. From a distance, she was stunning. But when she laughed she opened her mouth; a horrid mouth made of the hardest ice in the world. Everything, even her cone shaped teeth had an icy blue shine. If you were close enough you could see a dozen reflections of your own desperate gaze. Not a sight to see for the weak of heart. She could make anyone gasp for breath.

"Ah!" Pixie screamed. An intense cold pain ran up her arm all the way to her shoulder. Hela had wrapped her long fingers around her, squeezing her icy cold nails into her skin. The whole of Pixie's arm went numb and she could not wrestle it free.

"Let me go," she yelled.

But Hela just kept smiling at her like Pixie was a steak she was about to ingest. Her white skin reflected the prism colors from the stalactite giving her an eerie hue that contrasted sharply with her bright blue hair. Meni went to pounce on Hela. Her hand shot out, fingers pointing upwards, showing the palm of her hand. There was a sudden mist. When it finally dissipated, Meni was literally frozen in place, frost covering every inch of his now paper white skin. Pixie screamed. She could see his eyes moving inside the ice statue of his body.

"What have you done to him? Let go of him, please!" she pleaded with Hela.

"And let him ruin my plan? Tst, tst. That's just ridiculous!" she said, letting out a horrid cackle, like an old crow. Her mouth reflected the darkness overhead.

"Your plan is still ruined," Pixie said triumphantly. "I'm here, aren't I? When you release the breath it will reach me, not my mother."

She laughed; cold and carelessly like someone above all inconveniences. "Silly little Pixie Piper. You think it is a coincidence that I caught you? Tell me, how was I ever going to force your mother to marry my son? Threaten her with death? She would rather die than submit. It would have been pointless to demand anything without something to bargain with. Of course, when my spies informed me of your existence, the final piece of the puzzle fell into place. Now that you're here, I have just what I need to persuade your mother into the right kind of wedlock. After all, she would never place her precious little daughter in danger, would she?"

She smiled, batting her eyes coquettishly in hypocritical flattery. Then her face turned to ice and her smile faded, revealing a vicious sneer. The evil ice fairy let out a high-pitched whistle and in seconds, the room was filled with guards, most of them wingless fairies, although Pixie recognized several of the abominable snowmen Dalu had spoken of. They must've been about twenty feet tall, for their heads were almost invisible in the heavy mist near the ceiling. They were covered from head to toe in long white fur. She wondered how they could see anything behind so much hair and fog.

Actually, abominable snowmen, or yetis, can't see. Their eyes only picture shadows and silhouettes. Not that there's much to see when you live atop snow capped mountains. Instead, snowmen get around using their incredible sense of smell. Said to be better than any hound's, their noses can detect a seed sprouting several feet beneath earth and snow. They are vegetarians and rather mild mannered in nature, but when instigated they can turn into killers.

"Take them to the Treasure Room," Hela said. "It's time to release the breath."

Two of the regular guards took hold of Meni's frozen body and hoisted him up into the air. Hela handed Pixie's limp arm over to another pair of guards and they carried her off, out of the throne room and through the ice-cold corridors of Hela Winters' castle.

The treasure room was an enormous vault near the watchtower where Hela kept Garm's childhood trophies and all the other odd things he had collected from his many travels. They put them right next to an icy column with a snake carved around it. Pixie noticed a jar with her mother's name written on it. There was a golden smoky substance inside. It was probably the breath. It wasn't all lost. She could still breathe it into herself.

At that moment, Hela came through the door. She walked over to where they stood and waved her arms in a strange manner. Suddenly, a thin sheet of ice began to rise up from the floor. It circled around Pixie and Meni forming a seal against the column. They where locked in; airtight. She would never be able to catch the breath like this. She banged against the ice, but it was too strong. Pixie shot a desperate glance at Meni, as if somehow he could give her an answer, but Meni's eyes were already closed.

"Meni!" she yelled trying to shake him awake. "Wake up!" But it was useless. He was gone. Frozen.

20

Meni's Power

Pixie felt the last of her hopes disappear as Meni's eyes refused to open. Her friend, her only fairy friend, and Hela had destroyed him with a solitary hand. She banged her fists against the ice, lashing out all the insults she could think of. Nobody paid any attention. They were all staring at someone who had just walked into the room.

A striking wingless fairy walked towards her. He was tall and muscular, with a square jaw, and a bright smile. His hair was dark like the night and his eyes were a deep shade of purple. Pixie could only guess he was Garm, except he didn't really look evil to her. In fact, he was quite handsome and she wondered why her mother never took a liking to him.

He leaned against the cage, sizing Pixie up. "So this is Delmes' half-human brat?" he sneered. "Not much, is she, mother? The father must be a terrible sight. And who is this lovely piece of ice sculpture?" he said looking at Meni. "Mother you've outdone yourself. Look! He's already fallen into hypothermic state. There's no telling how long he can last like that." He smiled; a vicious cunning smile, aimed straight at Pixie. "You know Pixie, when his eyelids turn grey, that's when you can be certain he's gone for sure." His words emanated pure evil.

She felt a sudden heat rise up from her gut until she thought she would burst. Her fist struck the ice so hard the whole cage shook. Yet, there was not a crack or dent in the wall. Garm laughed deeply and with pure satisfaction. Now she could understand why her mother would run away from this. He was like a rotten smell in a garden of flowers; it ruins the whole experience.

"Now, let us find your mother. Shall we, Pixie?" he said turning away from her.

He walked over to the jar and stood in front of it. Hela removed the lid and Pixie watched horrified as the golden wisp of air flew upwards and out the hallway. Garm and everybody else followed, leaving Pixie all alone.

She felt like dying. Everything was over, ruined. She had failed. Her friend was gone. Her mother would be found. They would all be killed. She threw her arms around Meni's icy form and began to cry. Hot salty tears streamed down her cheeks and onto Meni's shoulders. She felt a strange comfort, like somehow he could feel her and was telling her everything would be all right.

Suddenly, steam began to spurt out of Meni's body. She backed away, terrified. The vapor was filling the cage turning it into a small sauna. She heard a loud crack. A large chunk of ice fell off of Meni's chest. There were a series of tiny cracks and she noticed his wings had defrosted. Her tears were melting the ice! Before long, Meni was standing in a pool of water, shaking from head to toe, his color a light shade of grey. Pixie squeezed him. He was alive! Her friend was still alive. Maybe there was still hope. She felt a pair of icy hands wrap around her wings.

"Th...th...thanks," he said, still looking slightly frozen. "How long was I gone?"

"Long enough to bring a smile to Mr. & Mrs. Cold out there," Pixie told him. "Bet they're planning where to put their new piece." She let him warm up for a moment, but she couldn't stall for long. They had to hurry. "Meni, they've already released mom's breath. We have to follow the trail and try to catch up with it. We haven't got much time."

He nodded quietly and tried to get up, but he was shaking so violently he couldn't even crawl. He folded his wings forward, stretching them all the way around his chest and head, until he was entirely shrouded inside them; like a cocoon. He began to glow, gathering intensity. Suddenly he exploded with bright golden light. It felt warm against Pixie's face and chest, but it blinded her completely. When Meni faded and she could see again, he was back to his normal color, his cheeks slightly flushed.

"What did you just do?" she asked.

"I healed myself," he said. "Just something

I discovered I could do, that's all."

"That's all? It looked pretty cool to me. How come you didn't teach me how to do that?" Pixie demanded.

"I wouldn't know if you could," he replied. "None of my friends can. It makes them a little nervous, so I try not to do it around them."

"But there was such a warm feeling all over the cage!" Pixie protested. "I don't see why anyone would mind."

"It just feels awkward being the only one who can do it," he explained.

"Wow!" Pixie exclaimed. "Back home, kids who are the only ones who can do something are always showing off. It gets annoying. My mom says you should be humble about your talents, but never embarrassed by them."

"You don't think it's strange, what I can do?" Meni asked.

"Are you kidding? I wish I could fix myself whenever I was having an asthma attack. I wouldn't miss out on anything. And my friends would probably all ask me to heal all their cuts and scrapes. Besides, I'm a half-human.

Remember? Strange is part of my description," she laughed.

"I guess you have a point," Meni said. "But forget about that now. We have to find a way out of this ice box. Did you say it was warm when I cocooned?" he asked.

"Yes. It was real cozy, like sitting by a lit fireplace," Pixie added.

"Then, come on," he said, pulling her closer.

He wrapped his wings around both of them, making sure everywhere was sealed. Then, without any kind of movement from him his wings burst into fiery light. Both their bodies began to glow intensely. Pixie closed her eyes. The light was too bright for her to see anything, but she felt strangely aware of her whole body. She felt the blood pumping from her heart into her veins and organs, dispersing heat across her body like it was somehow connected to Meni's light. Every breath she took filled her with energy. She could feel the air as it was absorbed in the lungs and carried through the bloodstream across every inch of her, tiny electric shocks that traveled down her spinal cord telling her legs to move or her fingers to clench.

Finally, Meni opened his wings and released her. The glow subsided and Pixie found the air in the cage seemed fresher than before. Something cold struck the top of her head and slithered between the strands of her hair until it reached her scalp. A piercing sensation ran down the length of her head. She looked up. Tiny drops of melted ice were sliding down the walls, forming a small puddle of freezing water on the floor. The cage was melting!

"Quick, bang on the walls!" Meni yelled.

They punched, kicked, pushed and shoved. Pixie even removed her shoe and threw it at the wall. After a while, a large crack formed. It grew bigger with every strike. At last, Meni managed to land a strong kick and the whole thing crumbled into a million pieces. They were free.

21

Catching A Breath

"Did you see where they went?" Meni asked when they were free of the cocoon.

"They went out that way," Pixie replied, pointing towards an arched doorway on the back wall.

Pixie and Meni made their way among the trinkets in the room. Pixie had never seen so many entirely useless things in one single place. It reminded her of the garage back home where her mother stashed anything she thought would come in handy in the future. The walls were lined with shelves containing all sorts of figurines, books and tiny ice boxes. On the floor, tables, chests and life-sized statues blocked their path so they were walking in a zigzag.

When they reached the archway there was no sign of the breath, Hela, or Garm. The hallway was a mess of doorways that lead to rooms with more doorways, which in turn lead to rooms with more doors and so on and so forth.

"The tower!" Meni said suddenly, stopping dead in his tracks.

"What?"

"If we get to the tower, we'll have a view of the whole crater and we can see which way the breath goes," Meni explained.

"Great idea, but how do we get to the tower?" Pixie asked.

"There has to be a stairwell somewhere," Meni said.

"Yea, but whe… Wait a minute!" Pixie said suddenly. "I remember seeing a long spiral staircase on the way to the Treasure Room. We have to go back through the room and go out the other way. I believe the stairs weren't that far."

"Are you sure, Pixie? Didn't you say they

headed THIS way?" he asked, pointing to the opposite end of the hall.

"Yes, Hela and Garm headed that way, but the stairs are this way. I'm sure," Pixie assured him.

She was right. They found a spiral stairwell just outside the first entrance to the treasure room. It was really long so they couldn't quite see the end of it. The ceiling was too short for flight, but at least it led them upwards to the possibility of an open landing or window where they could fly away.

"Quit stepping on my wings, will you?" Meni complained.

"Then tuck them in, they're drooping all over," she snapped back. The stress was starting to get to her and her pack kept getting heavier with every step she took. She changed it from one shoulder to another, but to no avail. If they didn't reach the top soon, her legs would certainly give way. They rounded the next bend. Pixie used her arms to push herself up. There was the platform. She slid across the floor instead of taking the last two steps and spread out panting.

It was the highest thing she had ever climbed.

The tower was edged into the southwest corner of the crater's mouth. You could see the whole length of the frozen lake to one side and all the way to the beach from the other. It was literally the highest point in all of Dahna. Even the air felt thinner up there. It was magnificent! Pixie wondered why Hela didn't build the whole castle up there instead of down in the crater. It would have proved a much better spot. But of course, Hela Winters would have never built her home so exposed to an attack. It was a possibility she always kept in mind. For those who do wrong tend to have many enemies. It is the way of life, human or otherwise.

"I don't see anyone down there," Meni said, scanning the surface below. "Maybe the breath hasn't left the building yet."

Just as Pixie took a peak, a golden haze flew out of an air vent near the middle of the crater. It did several twists and spirals until finally it found its course and began moving steadily upwards. A group of small dark figures quickly followed. One of them had a flowing head of blue hair. The breath was soon too high for Hela and Garm to follow on foot and neither of them had any wings. This was her chance. She leaped from the tower taking a deep dive towards the center of the volcano. It didn't take long for Hela's people to notice her. She left a golden purple glow unlike any other. Pixie saw a yeti throw something at her. It was coiled and completely white except for a pair of red eyes. She flew up to avoid getting hit just in time to miss two gigantic fangs lashing at her leg. It was an ice snake and it landed almost invisible on the frozen lake. A storm of more snakes and stones followed, but she was able to fly above them, concentrating on the string of air that was her ultimate goal.

She was only a few feet away when her mother's breath suddenly stopped in midair. It flipped several times in the same spot, leaning in each direction as if trying to catch a scent. Finally the golden smoke began moving straight in Pixie's direction. She leaned forward to increase her speed and meet it halfway, but a bolt of lightning cut her off.

Garm was standing atop a fast-moving gray cloud that he held in check with a pair of reigns.

Every time he stomped his foot on it a flash of lightning shot from underneath. She swerved and managed to avoid getting hit. The breath was still coming at her, but so were the electrical arrows from Garm's cloud. It was barely an arm's reach away. Just a couple more beats of her wings and she would make it. A sudden shadow fell over her. Garm was right on top of her, his leg raised, ready to land down hard against the cloud. She closed her eyes tight and begged for speed. When she opened them she was right upon the breath. The whiff of smoke spiraled in front of her and then flew into her nose. A cozy warm feeling filled her whole body, like she was safe inside her mother's arms. She'd done it! She'd caught the breath! In the excitement, she didn't hear Meni's warning shouts or see the flash of light announcing the bolt that was about to strike her on the back. Before she knew it, something was piercing into her shoulder blades. She heard the sizzling sound of burning flesh and then her body began to spasm uncontrollably. Her wings stiffened and she could no longer move them. With the first signs of free fall she lost all consciousness. The last thing she heard was

Garm's cruel laughter as his figure grew smaller the further down she fell.

22

Cold Dreams Come True

Pixie woke in the throne room with a searing pain on her head as Hela threw freezing water over her already bruised body. She glared at Pixie with a bucket in her hand and her lips clenched so tightly only a thin blue line ripped the whiteness of her skin. Pixie tried to move, to fly away, but her hands and feet had been tied to the wall by massive chains of ice and her wings were adhering to the wall as the water began to freeze over them.

"Go ahead," Hela said smiling viciously, "try and get out of that. Hopefully, you'll tear your wings out. It serves you right too. Your friend almost killed my Garm." She sneered and threw a bloody arrow at Pixie's feet. It was one of Meni's. Pixie was sure of it. Perhaps he'd gotten away.

"Where is he? What have you done to him?" Pixie demanded.

"That is none of your concern. Right now, I'm your biggest problem. You have put me in a very ugly position Pixie. I had a very simple plan. Violence hardly played a role in it. Now it seems I'm forced to use it against you. It almost makes me sad. Still, I WILL get my way no matter what must get done. Do you understand?" she said putting her face right up to Pixie's.

"What do you want?" Pixie shouted

"I want you to tell me where you live. That's all. Just give me your address."

"No," Pixie answered quickly. She knew all Hela wanted was to get to her mother.

"Then you leave me no choice."

The winter queen placed her pale hands on Pixie's face. They were so cold; they felt like they were made of ice. Pixie tried to turn away, but Hela tightened her grasp. She would not let Pixie move her head at all. She took a long deep breath. Then she closed her eyes and breathed on Pixie.

The cold air entered her body, freezing her lungs until they burned. She couldn't breathe. She couldn't move. Her chest refused to obey her no matter how many times she told herself to breathe. The seconds stretched on stealing the little air left in Pixie. Then she felt her ribs squeeze hard into her lungs and she began to cough. Her body arched forward and a large glob of phlegm landed right next to Hela's bare foot. The ice queen only smiled a little wider, pleased. When the coughing finally subsided Pixie felt like she'd been running for miles. With every breath she took she heard an all too familiar wheezing echoing through the walls.

"What's wrong Pixie? You can't breathe?" Hela asked in a high mocking pitch. "You see? Human blood is inferior to fairies'. They should never be mixed. Now, are you going to give me that address?" She looked calmer now. Like she was certain she would succeed.

"Never," Pixie said, looking right into her eyes.

Hela's face darkened into a bone gray. She took a step back from Pixie and raised her hand high above her head ready to strike, but instead she clenched her fist, digging her nails hard into the flesh of her hand. She glowered at Pixie and took another deep breath, holding it in for a second or two before exhaling. A dense fog filled with tiny particles of ice emerged from her mouth.

The air scraped the skin inside Pixie's nose as it entered her body. Her lungs were not just burning this time. They were in pain. The wheezing echoed through the walls in rapid successions as she struggled to breathe. Each time she inhaled, the wheezing was louder and less air came through. She was having an asthma attack. There was nothing she could do. She began breathing even faster, panic starting to rise up her chest and into her head. Suddenly, the wheezing stopped. There was absolutely no air going through. She looked desperately from side to side not sure if she was looking for something to help her escape or silently saying no to herself.

Her legs weakened and her knees gave in. She sunk into the floor hanging from the ice chains like wet laundry. She was on the verge of losing consciousness.

"You know? I can stop it. I can make it all go away. All you have to do is tell me where you live," Hela said, smiling viciously at Pixie.

Pixie closed her eyes again trying to stay calm. One, two, three, she counted silently, trying to breathe long and deep. But it was impossible with the inflammation in her lungs. Her head began to spin from lack of oxygen. Soon, she would pass out. It was probably best. That way, she would never be able to tell on her mother. So she accepted her fate and gave in to the shadows that engulfed her.

She was at home in her mother's arms. Golden brown locks that smelled of fresh coconuts tickled her nose as she pressed her face against Mrs. Piper's shoulder in a fierce hug. Her mom's soft hands caressed her face gently before she kissed Pixie on the forehead. It was the safest place to be. For a short moment, she forgot all about Hela Winters and her evil son Garm. She was home.

Suddenly there was a sharp cold sting as Hela's icy hand struck Pixie's face, scraping her cheek with her fingernails. She was being pulled away from her mother. The warmth and comfort of her home was gone. She was cold and hungry and the pounding on her head had become unbearable. She could hear Hela's voice far in the distance demanding to know where she lived and the wheezing still echoed loudly through the walls. She was overcome by the urge to be in her mother's arms again. Not in a dream, but in reality. She could not let Hela win. She had to fight it. She had to find a way to stop her asthma and get back home.

Pixie concentrated on her breathing again, trying to keep it as steady as possible. Slowly, each breath became deeper, until the wheezing stopped. Hela stared at her wide-eyed.

"I believe I've underestimated you Pixie Piper," Hela said through grinding teeth. "You are braver than most human girls I've come across. But no matter, I'll get what I want from you."

She breathed on Pixie again, but this time Pixie held her breath. The icy air glided across Pixie's face and spread outwards covering the chains in a soft white frost. She heard tiny cracks from the chains around her wrists and ankles. Without a second thought she pulled at the super-cooled chains. Her right hand came loose, showering Hela with tiny ice crystals. The snow fairy pointed her finger at Pixie's loose arm, shooting out a stream of bluish white ice. Pixie tucked her hand close to her body just as the ice brushed passed her and landed as a heap of chains on the floor behind her. She clenched her fist and tried to punch Hela in the face, but Hela stepped backwards and Pixie's fist landed on nothing but air. Instead, a rainbow burst forth from the ring on her finger. It hit Hela right between the eyes. The evil queen's white skin first turned purple, then blue, green and on through all the colors in the rainbow. Then she fell backwards and began convulsing on the ice.

Horrified, Pixie used the rainbow ring to free herself from the rest of the chains and made a run for it. She darted past the penguin pool, crossed the bridge and reached a grand double staircase. There was a large fountain at the base, but instead of spurting water it blew out fresh snow so that the whole of the room was drizzling with flakes like in a giant snow globe. The floor was covered in it and there were large three-toed foot prints headed up the stairs.

Pixie followed the footprints down a long corridor. There were all kinds of stuffed animals on the walls. A giant decapus eye rested on a shelf next to a long clawed tentacle. She felt chills run down her spine as she remembered her encounter with one just a few hours before. On the opposite wall there was the body of a beast with the tail and fins of a shark, but the head of an eel. Further along a giant turtle shell, so big she could fit her whole bed inside it, was sitting right in the middle of the floor.

Suddenly, she heard a scream. There was a growl and a hiss. It was coming from down the hall. She followed the sounds and found Meni fighting a yeti. One of his wings hung limply from his back. The ice on the floor seemed to slither and move slowly towards Meni's feet as one of the snowman's paws landed on his shoulder. She saw him tumble backwards and crash onto the floor. The ice seemed to gather speed, encircling him. The snowman raised its foot over Meni's face. It was going to crush him. Pixie shot a rainbow into the snow monster's eyes. It let out a screech and fell sideways. She glided across the floor and pulled Meni up. He was unconscious. With all her strength, Pixie tried to pull him up in the air. She managed to lift him off of the floor just as the moving ice reached the spot where Meni had lain. Dozens of ice snakes jumped and snapped at their feet as Pixie flew higher and higher. In the misty distance, she could see a light up ahead. It was probably one of the air vents. She flew upwards as fast as she could and closed her eyes, hoping it would be a way out.

23

A Way Out

The air became warmer as Pixie rose up and away from the ice snakes. She didn't dare open her eyes. There were probably bars or something. All of a sudden she felt the warm rays of the sun hit her face. She opened her eyes. They were out of the castle, but still deep inside the crater. She found a sheltered spot near the edge of the wall and set unconscious Meni down.

"Meni," she said tugging at his arm. "You have to wake up. I can't carry you all the way out of this crater. You have to help me."

"I can't move one of my wings," he finally

responded. "I think it's broken."

"Then heal yourself," she said to him casually.

"I can't," Meni said, trying to take hold of his wing so he could examine it. "With a broken wing, I can't make the cocoon."

"Oh! Meni, what are we going to do?" Pixie asked. They would never be able to climb out on foot.

"It's ok. It's just one of the hind wings. I can still fly and get some height. However I might need some help taking off and I don't think I will be able to steer well. Just give me a pull and don't let go of me, all right?"

"Are you sure?" Pixie asked, biting her lower lip. She always did the same thing when she wasn't sure of her decisions.

"No doubt about it, now let's go," he said getting up and shaking the snow off of his clothes.

They jumped up and flew away. Meni was able to fly almost without any help at all. Soon they were back at the rainbow highway. The bright lusty forest of Dahna lay ahead, inviting them back home. Pixie looked behind her at the old volcano, still not certain how they had managed to get out of there. She wondered whether or not Hela had survived the rainbow. Her convulsing body had not been a pleasant sight. And her son; she had mentioned something about Meni and her son.

"What happened to Garm?" Pixie asked Meni.

"I shot him with my bow and arrow," he said triumphantly tapping his pack where he kept his weapon of choice. "After you fell, I shot him in the shoulder and he fell; then the whole floor swarmed with snowmen and you both disappeared. I snuck back in the castle through the tower and was trying to find you when I ran into 'snowy' back there. Thanks by the way."

"Anytime," she said with a wink.

* * *

Dalu was waiting for them at the end of the rainbow. His face was swollen from having slept for twenty hours straight and he gnawed at his left fingernails as he glanced nervously from side to side.

"Pixie, Meni, you made it!" he said, rushing over and hugging Pixie fiercely. "I was so worried. I came here as soon as I woke. Let me see you, are you all right?" He spun her around and inspected her from top to bottom. There was an ugly abrasion on her leg where the decapus had caught her. "So there was a decapus!" Dalu exclaimed taking a closer look at Pixie's wound. "I knew it."

"You knew?" Pixie asked, pulling forcefully away from him.

"Well, I had my suspicions," Dalu said scratching his head, "so I went down to the library to check it out when I got bit by that jellyfish. I'm sorry Pixie, but I'm afraid I'm getting a little old. Not as quick to react as I used to be," he added.

"Did the guards ever find the spy?" Pixie asked him.

"Oh yes," Dalu said matter-of-factly. "He was trying to escape through the underground root system. Of course he denies everything, but we found his dust all over the jar with the jellyfish. The poor chap's been shaking his wings all day.

He's scheduled to be pupated tonight," he added, gently pulling a leaf from the tangled mass of Pixie's hair. Then he turned to Meni and noticed his broken wing. "Oh dear, we're going to have to get that fixed right away. Come with me." And he led them back to the Royal Tree.

24

Honors of the Seelie Court

"There, all done. You look beautiful Ms. Pixie," Tilly said when she finished dressing Pixie in the complicated flower dress. There was to be a big dinner party in her and Meni's honor.

"Thanks for coming to my rescue again," Pixie said, looking at Tilly through the full-length mirror of the dressing room. She hadn't noticed Tilly's purple eyes before.

"You must be happy to be getting back home," she said, keeping her head down in her customary fashion. "Is it very different from here?"

"Oh, yes. I don't think anywhere on earth

is like this," Pixie replied.

"I have never been outside of Dahna," she mumbled in an almost inaudible tone.

"Really?" Pixie asked turning around to look at her. "Why not?"

Tilly shrugged her shoulders, then finally raised her head and fixed her sparkling purple eyes on Pixie's. "I guess I wouldn't know where to go," she said.

"Then you must come visit me in Gardenville," Pixie suggested. She thought she saw a smile begin to curl on Tilly's mouth, but it was difficult to tell since she was looking down at the floor again.

"Best be off, Ms. Pixie, you don't want to be late this time," she said gently leading her into the garden.

Meni was waiting for her by the mushroom table. He was dressed in a deep blue tuxedo with ripples of water that moved as he walked. His wing was mended and placed on a sling to keep it from dragging on the floor.

"Hey, I'm glad you're here," Meni said. "I was beginning to think I would have to go through this thing by myself. Is it true we're having dinner with the whole Seelie Court?"

"Yes it is young man," said a melodious voice. It was the Queen. She was standing by the entrance dressed in a long gown of pearlescent white silk. Her long shimmering white hair was loose over her shoulders. The rainbow highlights gave color to the gown as she walked in and out of the shadows. "I wanted to thank you, Meni, for saving my granddaughter's life."

Meni bowed his head, much like Tilly had done to Pixie, and said something unintelligible.

"I will not forget all the kindnesses you have shown to Pixie," Ceres said to him raising Meni's chin up with her hand and looking straight into his eyes. "Now, let's all go to the feast."

She led them down the hall where Dalu was waiting for them dressed in a blue moss tuxedo. They went down four flights to the first floor and turned left. There was a pair of thick wooden doors almost three stories high carved with lotus flowers and birds. Two fairy guards pulled at massive ropes attached to the door handles. Slowly, the gigantic doors began to open and a warm ray of light peaked through the crack.

The long hall was set with sixteen tables divided into four groups of four where the members of the Seelie court sat already enjoying their appetizers. They all stopped eating and turned to stare at Pixie and Meni. Ceres nudged them forward. They walked bashfully down the middle of the room to a big table in the back set perpendicular to the others. There was a dead silence, not even a whisper. When they reached the table, Ceres turned them around to face the Court. Everyone began to clap and cheer. A blonde fairy dressed in a whitish transparent gown bowed at Pixie and then burst into the most beautiful song Pixie had ever heard.

"Who is that?" she asked her grandmother.

"That is Ariel, the Queen of the wind fairies," she replied, nodding at Ariel in the distance. "She is singing about the honor she feels to be in your presence." Pixie smiled at her and the wind fairy's voice did a crescendo until it overwhelmed the entire room.

After the song, waiters served them a marvelous seven-course fairy meal. Pixie and

Meni devoured their plates. They had hardly eaten anything during the journey. When finally the dessert plates where taken away Ceres rose from her throne and faced the congregation again. Dalu hurried over to her side, carrying a small square box and shaking all over.

"Fairies of the Seelie Court," Ceres began. "For the bravery and loyalty shown in saving a royal heir, I award Epimenides Treebark the Seelie Court Medal of Honor."

Loud cheers erupted from the crowd. In the front row, a small group of fairies rose from their benches clapping louder than the rest. They were Meni's parents, with all his brothers and sisters. Their eyes beamed as Meni walked dumbfounded towards the Queen to receive his medal.

After the ceremony they hovered about him each trying to hug him and congratulate him in their own way. Mr. Treebark was looking at Meni with the deep pride Pixie had seen when she had dinner at their house.

"Ask them," she told Meni, nudging him with her elbow.

"Ask them what? What are you talking about?" he looked at her confused.

"The F. E. X. Games," she said. "There's no way they'll say no now."

Meni bashfully approached his dad. Pixie saw him say something to Mr. Treebark's ear and a few seconds later there was a smile on both their faces. She knew he had said yes. There was no doubt in her mind. The rest of the family surrounded Meni, each member giving their own special advice. Pixie was enjoying the scene when Dalu conspicuously grunted next to her.

"Pixie," he began, pulling her aside from the commotion. "It's time to say good bye. We have to get you back home before your mother wakes up."

Pixie walked over to Meni. "I have to go," she told him, wishing she could take him with her. It would make her days much more enjoyable.

"Don't worry, Pixie," he said, as if reading her mind. "I'll send bee messages as often as possible. And you can always come visit me, anytime you wish."

She smiled, wondering if that would really

be possible. "Good bye," Pixie said hugging him. Then, she took Dalu's hand and left Meni with his family.

They went to the beach and pushed one of the leaf boats that lay on the sand into the water. Soon they were riding the green current back to the brook in the forest beside the school. The boat stopped near a large rock and Dalu sprinkled dust over the both of them. They were big again. The brook was only a trickle of water left from the rain, and the boat only an averaged sized leaf.

As they emerged from the forest Pixie saw the dark grey clouds above. It looked just like before she left. The red mustang convertible was still parked in front of the tree with the bright orange flowers. When they got back to her house the streets were deserted. Pixie jumped out of the car like she was allergic to it and ran for the door. Dalu's driving had somehow managed to get worse in the two weeks he was out of practice.

"Thank you Dalu," she said giving him one last hug. Then she looked up at the sky again. The clouds were low and dark. She let out a deep sigh before turning to open the door. It was back to spending boring rainy days indoors.

"You know Pixie?" Dalu said brightening his glow. "If you cast a rainbow on a cloudy day, the sun will come out." He winked at her and then turned around and walked towards the car. By the time Pixie could react, there was no sign of Dalu or the car. She hadn't heard an engine roar, or tires screech. Not even the door slam closed.

Back inside, her mother still slept comfortably in her bed. She had hardly stirred at all since Pixie left. There was a wide comfortable smile on her face. It made Pixie feel warm and proud. She had helped keep that smile there. Suddenly, the clock in the kitchen struck seven and Mrs. Piper flipped herself around facing Pixie. She heard the sound of a car pulling into the driveway. Her father was home from his meeting. She quickly tucked her wings into her back and ran down the stairs right before her father opened the door.

"I'm home," Mr. Piper announced. "What the...?" he said, noticing the golden purple dust all over the floor. "Darn! The ceiling must be shedding again!"

Pixie just gave him a big bright smile.

ABOUT THE AUTHOR

Maricel Jiménez Peña lives in Puerto Rico where she was born and raised. A love of fantasy, myth, and reading sparked the writer inside and she has been creating fantastical adventures ever since. Of course, no adventure in a book can ever compare to the real adventures with her two main characters in life: her boys.

41665431R00106

Made in the USA
Lexington, KY
21 May 2015